STEELE RESOLVE

A HAWKE FAMILY STORY

BILLIONAIRES OF NEW ORLEANS: THE HAWKE
FAMILY
BOOK 6

GWYN MCNAMEE

STEELE RESOLVE by
Gwyn McNamee © 2019

Cover Design: Michelle Johnson at Blue Sky Designs

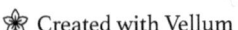 Created with Vellum

Love is love.

ACKNOWLEDGMENTS

Thank you to everyone who helped with Byron and Luca's story. I have been waiting five books to finally be able to give Byron a story, and it's exactly what I always pictured.

To my betas, thank you for providing invaluable feedback.

And to my husband and daughter for always supporting my writing.

PROLOGUE

BYRON

The damn lighting in the bar has me squinting at the menu in my hand to try to read the words. They blur together into black blobs on the cream paper, and a dull ache forms in my temples.

Fuck. I give up.

I hold the menu out to the bartender and wave my hand. "Just give me a burger and whatever IPA you have on tap."

The bottles behind the bar glow from the backlighting— green, red, brown, clear—and they actually have a really good liquor selection, but if I start hitting the hard stuff now, I'll have a rough morning tomorrow. I need to be at the club early to accept deliveries and get ready for the hustle that always is Saturday night, so I can't afford to be hungover as hell in the a.m.

This is my first Friday off in a long time, and I want to enjoy it. Just...not too much.

A few beers and hopefully a good fuck will be just what I need to unwind from everything that's been going on.

The bartender nods before turning his back to put my order in at the register.

I spin around on my stool to examine the place. The only other time I've been here, I was pretty lit, so I don't remember much, but I like the vibe of the place.

It's my kind of bar. Pool table in the corner. Dart boards along the far wall. High-top tables with stools and a line of dark booths wrapped in red leather. Low-key, almost a dive even though it's relatively new.

It was definitely designed to feel like a local neighborhood place, totally unlike so many of the other gay bars and clubs here. I get enough of the pumping bass music and flashing lights at the Hawkeye Club. When I'm off the clock, I don't want to deal with that. I just want to relax and unwind and maybe get off.

Is that really so much to ask?

Sure seems like it lately.

Ever since Ben and Caleb were killed, things have been tense at the club.

Understandably so.

Though Dom is dead, it doesn't feel like this is over. Stone's revelation and all the truths exposed were too much to take. And the decision to rebuild THREE at all, let alone at the same location, is agonizing for everyone. But since determining to move ahead, Savage and Gabe are once again swamped with construction on top of dealing with the loss of Ben—their best friend and Storm's husband. Everyone is struggling.

I pick up the slack where I can to help, and so does Vance over at TWO, but I needed this night off badly. A night where I don't need to think about schedules and staffing, paychecks and deliveries, customers and complaints. A few hours just about *me*.

When was the last time I even got laid?

Faces. Names. Dicks.

They float through my head in a haze, none of them particularly memorable or anything I'd want to repeat. Fun is fun, but it rarely leads to anything more permanent. Not that I'm looking for that tonight. Really, fun is about all I can handle right now.

Good times and bad decisions.

But eventually, down the road, settling down isn't out of the question.

If I can ever find anyone I connect with the way the Hawkes have, someone who looks at me with the same love and admiration they all do with their significant others, that will be the day these bars lose their appeal. But that day is not today.

The door to the bar swings open, bringing in a gust of warm evening air and my biggest dream and worst nightmare all wrapped up in one package.

Tall. Dark. Broody.

Devilishly handsome in gray jeans, a crisp white button-down shirt, and a black blazer perfectly cut to show off his defined chest, shoulders, and arms.

My fucking kryptonite.

Who is this guy?

Despite the size of New Orleans, the gay community always feels painfully small. Everyone knows everyone. Everyone's done everyone or knows someone else who has. And this isn't the type of bar tourists looking to have a good time flock to. Which makes the mystery man even more intriguing.

He's different. Shadowy and a bad decision waiting to happen.

A black, stormy gaze meets mine from across the room, and he zeroes in on me like an eagle circling his prey. Goosebumps break out across my exposed arms, and the corner of my mouth curls up.

"Here you go, man."

I jerk my head back to the bartender as he slides a cold pint of beer across the bar.

He flashes me a knowing grin. "Your burger will be up soon."

"Thanks."

Totally busted.

But I'm sure it's not anything new for him. Despite the low-key vibe in this place, pick-ups happen everywhere. It's just part of the life.

The stool next to me squeals against the worn planks of the wood floor as it's dragged out. My shoulders tense, and I curl my hand around the frosty glass. I take a drink, letting the crisp, hoppy liquid douse the heat his look sparked.

Don't look over. Stay cool.

Throwing yourself at him and asking him to suck your dick would be a bit of overkill. Not very gentlemanly, either. And if nothing else, I'm respectful even with my cock straining painfully against the zipper of my jeans.

He settles next to me and nods to the bartender. The scent of leather and rich, spicy aftershave washes over me. "Ardbeg single malt, please."

Damn.

The man smells incredible and knows good Scotch. Two more marks in the *perfect for me, so probably a bad idea* column.

I peek at him out of the corner of my eye, and a sly grin tilts his perfect lips. A grin that says he can read my mind and is arrogant enough to expect my attraction.

He nods toward my beer. "You just starting tonight or just ending?"

I force myself to fully meet his gaze. "Just starting."

The bartender pours the stranger's drink in front of us and pushes the tumbler toward him.

Long fingers curl around the glass. He turns on his stool and offers a smirk that has my cock twitching. "Me too."

He raises his drink to me. Dark eyes I could drown in twinkle in amusement, and he arches a brow at me. "To new beginnings."

I return his smile and struggle not to use my free hand to reach down to adjust my cock. "To new beginnings."

Our glasses clink together.

My evening just got a lot more interesting.

STEELE

I never thought I'd be back in New Orleans. I never thought there would be any reason to be here. But here I am, in the city I swore I'd never return to, taking over a business that killed my sperm donor, at a bar that could expose the biggest secret in my life and put my life at risk—again.

Shit.

I should have learned my lesson in Philly. This isn't something I can be openly. Not in this life. Not in this job. Not in this city where I'm making my new home.

But I'm greedy and selfish, and I couldn't stop myself from coming out tonight, from seeking companionship, release, connection. Even bad guys deserve that. This will be the last time I'm going to get to indulge in a little fun if I want any chance at still maintaining my anonymity. It's only a matter of time before people realize who I am and what I'm doing back here. People who could cause a lot of trouble for me.

I barely got out of Jersey alive, and I'm not about to start another war here. The vultures have already circled and moved in to feast on the carcass of the Abello empire, and if I don't step up and act soon, there will be nothing left to save.

Lying low has permitted me the opportunity to observe the lay of the land and to find out how my old friends, the Hawkes have been dealing with the fallout of dear ol' Dad's actions, but I can only remain concealed for so long.

Tonight, I'm not thinking about that. Tonight, in this place, is about enjoying the little bit of time I do have and finding an outlet for the stress and tension coiled in my body. Months of watching my back. Meetings I wasn't sure I would walk out of alive. Very real threats being hurled at me. Barrels of guns pointed at my face. It starts to weigh on you.

This is a new city. A new day. A new life.

And the second I walked through that door, I knew the big, broad-shouldered man, now sitting next to me at the bar, with his tattoos and muscles bulging under his t-shirt, was going to be my entertainment for the night.

I take a sip of Scotch. The smoky peat warms my chest. "Are you a local?"

The guy lifts his tattooed arm to bring his glass to his lips and takes a sip of his beer before turning to face me. "I am. You?" A dark eyebrow quirks up as he waits for my response.

I chuckle and swirl the amber liquid in my glass. "I am now, but I'm from the East Coast."

He gives me a lopsided grin and chuckles. "Figured. The accent gives you away."

I tip my head back and laugh. "I never really considered myself as having much of an accent."

One of his broad shoulders rises and falls. "Maybe that's because you were up there, not down here."

"I was actually born here, but it's been a couple decades since I've been back." And I probably never would have come this far south again if Gabe hadn't taken out the man I once called Dad and if I hadn't been outed to the crew in Jersey.

New Orleans has never been home. It's just the place I was born, a place where the only good memories stem from the Hawkes. Our house was in a constant state of turmoil—Mom and Dad arguing about one thing or another. His work. His mistresses. Him not wanting the embarrassment of a gay son.

The Hawkes were more a family to me than my own, and when we left, it was both a huge relief to be getting away from the man who sired me and agonizing to know I would probably never see them again. And now, after what he did, the chances of them welcoming me back into the fold with open arms is almost nil.

So, I'll look for other arms. Even if it's just for one night.

My companion raises his eyebrows and nods as he takes another drink. "So, what brings you back? Business or pleasure?"

Hopefully both.

"Work and some personal business."

Which are inextricably intertwined.

They are also the last things I want to discuss right now.

I've always hated small talk. Why can't we just cut the pretense and get down to business instead of pretending we care? These formalities, the games played to try to eliminate feeling shady about yourself in the morning, they are pointless in the end.

An escort would be much easier. No risk of a personal connection. But that's never been an option. There's too much of a chance of blackmail if anyone ever discovers who I am. People who will take money for sex will demand money for silence. And while I don't lack money, I do lack patience for idiots who think they can get away with trying to out me.

So, anonymous bars and sort-of fake names have always been the way to go. And it worked for a long time, until Philly.

I hold out my hand to him. "Steele Clemenza."

Not a name anyone will know or connect to Luca Abello—the man about to revive his father's criminal empire from the ashes.

He takes it with a firm grip and shakes. A spark of electricity rolls up my arm, down through my torso, and straight to my dick.

Christ.

The corner of his mouth tilts up. He felt it, too.

"Byron Harris. It's nice to meet you."

I give him the grin that's always worked so well for me in the past. It's one of my best assets and something I'm sure to pull from my arsenal whenever it's needed. "You too."

The bartender reappears with a plate containing a burger and fries and sets it in front of Byron. "Here's your burger. Can I get you anything else?"

My stomach rumbles, and I nod toward his plate. "Can I get one of those, too?"

I hadn't even realized how hungry I am, but suddenly, looking at Byron and his rippling tattooed muscles, plump lips, and dark eyes, I'm positively ravenous.

1

ONE MONTH LATER

BYRON

The doors of the Hawkeye Club swing open, and I lean against the bar to brace myself for the hurricane about to blow in. One with the last name Abello.

But the one who walks in wrapped in a suit, perfectly tailored to show off his muscular form and to tell anyone who sees it he means business—deadly business—isn't Luca Abello. It's Steele.

What the hell?

Landon freezes where he sits in front of me at the bar and clenches his jaw.

Why would he react to Steele like that?

My chest tightens. My throat constricts. My vision blurs.

All the pieces click together. What Steele told me that night at the bar...

"I was actually born here, but it's been a couple decades since I've been back..."

"Work and some personal business."

Jesus, what have I done?

Steele *is* Luca.

The man flashes me a sly smile—one that freezes my blood. He doesn't look at all surprised to see me.

He knew. He fucking knew.

He wanders over to the bar and sidles up next to Landon. "Landon, I didn't know you were going to be at the meeting."

Landon shakes his head. "I didn't even know about it. I just came for a drink." He tilts his bottle toward the man whose bed I was in only weeks ago.

Luca nods and scans the club. "Where are they?"

Shit.

If I don't pull myself together, Landon is going to know something's going on.

I shake my head, clear my throat, and nod toward the elevator. "Upstairs. Savage's office. Take the elevator. First door on the left. I'll call up to let them know you're here."

With all the cameras covering this place, they already know, but I'll call anyway. It will give me something to do to avoid looking at Luca any longer than necessary.

Luca nods and taps the top of the bar. "Thanks."

He throws me a wink before he casually pushes away from the bar and saunters over to the elevator. The doors open, and he steps inside. He turns and flashes me a knowing grin before the doors slide closed in front of him.

I grab the phone with a shaky hand and press the button for Savage's office.

Savage grunts a greeting. "That him?"

"Yeah, he's here."

The man whose father killed Ben and Caleb. The man who has been stalking Storm. The man who is the new head of the damn mob in New Orleans. The man who is evil incarnate. The man I've slept with.

Savage growls. "Fucking asshole. Tell Landon to come join us if he would like to be involved in the meeting."

My eyes flick over to Landon's. "Yeah, okay. Thanks." I drop the phone back to the receiver. "Savage says if you want to join them, go ahead."

Landon considers the offer for a minute while my heart thunders.

How could I have been so stupid? Literally sleeping with the fucking enemy.

Sweat beads on my brow, and I reach up and wipe it away.

I have to get out of here.

Landon shakes his head. "I think I'll stay here and have another beer."

I nod and pop the top off another IPA for him. "That may be the wisest choice, man. You don't want to be in the middle of anything involving that many Hawkes in one room." Especially when they're all pissed off and have a viper in there with them. "I need to go check on something."

Any excuse to get the fuck out of here. I rush down the back hallway past the girls' changing room to the tiny employee bathroom at the rear of the club. The door clicks shut behind me, and I lean against it and drop the back of my head to the hard surface.

Fuck. Fuck. Fuck. Fuck. What the fuck have I done?

I step forward and kick the cabinet under the sink. My foot goes straight through the wood. "Shit."

Add this to the list of things I've fucked up.

I yank my foot out, bend down, and examine the damage. I'm going to have to replace this and figure out a way to explain it to the guys. But it's the least of the things I need to worry about.

Of all the stupid shit I've done in my life, sleeping with Steele...

Shit.

Sleeping with *Luca* has to be the biggest.

The sworn enemy of the only family I have ever had was in

my bed. Was inside me. I let him waltz right into my life and, by association, theirs.

Jesus, what did I tell him?

Everything we said to each other that night rushes back in one giant blur. I told him I worked at a strip club. He thought it was funny.

Did he ask questions about them?

I rise to my feet and scrub my hands over my face. I can't remember. The beer and Scotch and lust created a foggy haze over the entire conversation. I had other things on my mind—like getting back to his place.

He must have asked about them, right?

The only explanation for any of this was it was a set up from the beginning. He knew exactly who I was when he walked into that bar. He was on a mission to spy on the Hawkes.

He fucking set me up.

I should've known something was fishy. A guy like that strolling in and being interested in a guy like me. The watch he wore cost more than my car. He was slumming it from the second he stepped foot in The Back Pocket, but I fell for it hook, line, and sinker. Dark eyes and the flash of a smile was all it took for me to open myself up to him.

Am I that fucking desperate for affection that I let the devil himself walk right into my bed?

Apparently so.

"How do I tell Savage and Gabe? How the hell do I tell Storm and Landon? Stone, or Nora, or Dani? How do I tell any of them?" My voice echoes around the tiny tiled room. No answers come.

I crank on the faucet and splash the ice-cold water on my face, letting it run down my neck and the front of my shirt. It doesn't help. Not one fucking bit.

My hand shakes as I reach for a paper towel.

Get your shit together, Byron.

I can't go back out there like this. They'll know something's up. There are far more important things to worry about than me right now, like the fact that man is upstairs and in Savage's office right now.

I just need to keep my cool and keep my shit together for a little while longer. Long enough to figure out how to tell the Hawkes what I've done. Long enough to come up with a plan.

STEELE/LUCA

The ride down in the elevator to the main floor of the Hawkeye Club seems far slower than the ride up, but that may just be because I'm anticipating seeing Byron again. I lean back against the wall of the elevator car and watch the numbers drop from two to one. The doors slide open to bumping bass music and a girl wrapped around the pole.

Her long, pale legs caress the shiny steel, and she swings around it, her red hair streaming out like a halo and brushing along the stage.

She's incredibly talented, and really, quite beautiful. Even if she isn't my type, I can't help but appreciate a stunning woman when I see one. She's exactly the sort of woman I used to keep on my arm before...when I bothered to try to create the illusion of a "normal" relationship, so I wouldn't be discovered. She may not be my pick, but she'd make a truly gorgeous trophy for any man.

Now, onto my type...

I slowly make my way across the floor and scan the club for a very specific set of broad shoulders. Ones I vividly remember squeezing between my hands as I pounded into him that night. But Byron is suspiciously absent from the bar where I left him stunned less than an hour ago.

The massive black guy who's been stuck to Storm like glue recently scowls at me from where he's perched on a stool. His dark eyes follow me, and I flick him a wave and a grin. The guy is just doing his job. There's no need to be anything but courteous. As long as he doesn't interfere with my business, there's no need to be enemies.

Too bad no one else seems to be able to see that.

I stroll past the man at the door, who gives me a sneer that's probably meant to intimidate and ensure I get the message that I'm not welcome.

No worries.

I don't have any plans on returning to The Hawkeye Club until my old friends are willing and ready to talk more and consider renewing our relationship.

If that ever happens.

A light drizzle falls from a pitch-black night sky as I make my way to the car. It fits my darkening mood.

Though, I can't say I'm surprised by the outcome of my meeting with the Hawkes. No matter what our history might be, it's impossible for them to overlook who my father was and what he did. And I can't say I blame them.

The man was brutal. The man was harsh. The man was petty and fucking heartless. And I'm his flesh and blood, no matter how much I'd rather forget that.

The only time I ever saw him give anyone real, true affection was to Antonia Hawke and her children. He certainly never showed it to Mom or me. He had a soft spot for their family, especially after Sam's death, yet, he still turned on them. He still made the business his number one priority.

He may have tried to explain it away as protecting Stone, but everyone knows that's bullshit. He was protecting himself. He needed Stone and couldn't lose him. It was never about helping someone else; it was about the man helping the only one who mattered to him—himself.

What he did isn't so easily forgotten, and I'm nothing but a reminder for them. One they'd rather not have to face.

I slide into the Maybach and fire it up. The engine rumbles, but rather than tear out of the lot, I pull out my phone.

Nothing from Byron.

It shouldn't be a surprise, but I had hoped to find a message from him now that he knows who I really am. Perhaps a request to meet to talk. A request that undoubtedly would lead to more if I have my way.

Byron is one of the sexiest men I've ever met. His dark, dominant presence. His ability to stand his ground with me without a hint of hesitation or backing down. No one stands toe to toe with Luca Abello without flinching. It was impressive. And the way we fit so perfectly together...

I shake my head and back out of the parking spot. He probably needs time to process. And as annoying as that may be, I understand it. The look on his face when I walked in...the poor man was white as a sheet. I thought he might pass out.

He never expected to see Steele again. Certainly not in his domain and definitely not with another name. One he knows so well. And one he undoubtedly has connected with negative feelings. He knew Ben and Caleb, too. He's close with Stone and the Hawkes like they're family.

If he had known who I was when we met, I likely would have ended up with a drink in my face if I were lucky, and a fist there if he were doing what he really wanted.

My reputation precedes me. Even if he weren't tied inextricably to the Hawkes, Byron would have judged me the moment I said "Abello." The same way everyone else in my life has. Whether it was here in New Orleans as a child, or when Mom and I fled to Jersey, that name brought baggage with it I always hoped and tried to shed.

No such luck.

I tighten my hands on the wheel and peel out of the parking lot toward the Ritz-Carlton.

Seeing Byron tonight may have ruined any chance of ever

being with him again in the way I so desperately crave. The only good thing about coming to the club was I got to speak my peace, even if the Hawkes didn't want to hear it.

And they *really* didn't want to hear it.

It stings they so easily believe the worst of me. That they're so quick to think I would only come back to hurt them or that I would wish them any harm. They so easily forgot what we had as children. The friendship. The camaraderie. The trust.

I didn't expect the red carpet to be rolled out for me after twenty years and everything that's happened in that time, yet I had hoped they would be a little bit more reasonable about listening to an old friend.

It may have been asking too much. But I spoke from the heart, and that's really all I could do. I've laid all the cards on the table, and it's now up to the Hawkes to determine how to play them.

The rain falls harder now, pelting the windshield and slickening the road beneath me. I press the gas pedal, and the car flies through the wet streets.

Speed. The feeling of teetering just on the edge of control. The desire to push harder, go faster...

It's the only thing that will fill the void in my chest right now. One created by the double rejection tonight. I'm willing to give the Hawkes and Byron some space to consider their next moves.

Maybe they just need a cooling off period.

Showing up the way I did at Storm's office the other day undoubtedly shook them. They need to digest the fact that I'm back. Once the dust settles, hopefully, my friends will return to me.

And as for Byron...

"Fuck." I slam my hand against the steering wheel.

That man will be nothing but trouble, yet I know I won't stay away long. He's not the type of person you forget so easily.

In the meantime, I have business to attend to.

2

LUCA

The man sitting across from me appears innocuous enough, almost like an older, kind Hispanic uncle or neighbor, but I've been in this business long enough to know looks can be deceiving. This man is lethal. He also has an agenda he very much wants to continue here in New Orleans. One my presence is going to impede upon. He almost took out dear old Dad before Gabe did, so he's a very real danger to me, despite his outward appearance.

Their turf war played a huge part in the violence happening during that unfortunate time not so long ago. The man swept into New Orleans in the wake of Katrina and set up shop when there was turmoil and people to take advantage of.

He was smart then. I can't say the same of him now. Which is precisely why I extended him this...*invitation*.

I flash him a grin and nod toward him where he sits in the chair in front of my desk. "I'm so pleased you could meet with me today, Mr. Castillo."

He snorts and sits up straighter, trying to make his diminutive frame seem more intimidating. "I didn't have much choice, did I, Mr. Abello? Or should I say, Mr. Clemenza?"

Smartass.

I may have tried to use Mom's maiden name when we lived in Jersey to avoid all the trappings that came along with the Abello moniker, but he knows full well that I am back to being an Abello now that I've returned to New Orleans. It's not something I can escape, no matter how hard I try, so it's time to embrace it. That decision was made and final before I ever stepped off the plane here.

He's trying to rattle me. Attempting to get me riled up so I'll make a mistake. I don't make mistakes. At least, not in business.

My actions in Baltimore outed me to my Jersey family and killed any chance I had of continuing to climb the ranks there. That was a personal matter that, unfortunately, oozed into the other side of my life. They would have killed me if I hadn't been quick and intelligent enough to offer them something they could only get from me—a piece of the NOLA territory formerly controlled by the Abellos.

Having to send a chunk of my earnings to Jersey isn't ideal, and it grates on every nerve I have, but sometimes, uncomfortable arrangements are necessary to accomplish your end goals. I don't have the strength or backing to do anything rash like take them out, so for now, it's a necessary reminder of my former life there.

But I'm not going to let Castillo rattle me.

I'm here. I'm in charge. I'm alive.

Those three things are priceless.

I recline in the huge leather chair behind my desk, the same desk the former Abello sat behind when he ran his empire from this room. The same desk that sat between Castillo and him when they met a mere year ago.

A blink of an eye in the grand scheme of things, yet so much has happened since then, it feels more like an eternity. And Castillo has used every second of it to advance his interests.

"I know you're a busy man, Mr. Castillo, so I won't keep you long. Let's get right down to business. You seem to think that because my father is gone, that means his territory is yours. Unfortunately, that is not accurate."

He chuckles and leans forward. "Your father's dead. It's been over six months. No one stepped up to claim this." He raises his hands, waves them, and lets them fall. "I was well within my rights to take over."

I let his words hang in the air between us for a moment. He needs time to consider how asinine and stupid they are. He shifts uncomfortably in his seat while I stare him down.

The longer you let someone sweat, the more impact your words will have when you do speak. It's one thing I learned being the son of Dom Abello, one of the very few things the old man taught me—before he disowned me—that has actually helped me advance in life.

I finally offer him a slow smile. "Wrong. It is rightfully mine, and I'm here to claim it." He opens his mouth to object, but I raise my hand to silence him. "I have been here for weeks, watching, getting the lay of the land, figuring out where people stood, where we stood. And now, I'm letting you know how it is."

He snarls. "You think you can just waltz in here like that? Who the fuck do you think you are?"

"I'm Luca Abello, and I'm here to take back what's mine. If you want to stand in my way, then you will pay the price." It's as simple and direct as I can put it.

His nostrils flare, and his clenched jaw tics. He flexes his fists on the armrests of the chair. "Is that a threat?"

I grin and watch his face redden. The man's anger is humorous. He's been in this business longer than I've been alive, yet he still doesn't understand the realities of it. There may have been an opening, some perceived weakness somewhere in the Abello empire when my sperm donor was at the helm, but there isn't one now.

I won't make the same mistakes.

"I don't make threats. I make promises. Ones I always follow through on. So, if I were you, I would strongly reconsider your stance. Your disagreement with my father almost ended badly for both of you. I would hate to see you go the way he did, but I'm more than willing to do it if necessary."

I wasn't lying when I told the Hawkes I'm not Dom Abello. I don't hurt innocent people. But Castillo is far from innocent, and sometimes a little head bashing and smashing of kneecaps is necessary to get across a point. Other times, something a little more permanent has to occur to really send the right message.

Castillo jerks to his feet, his hands clenched at his sides. "Your father thought he was untouchable, and he died sitting in the exact same place you now occupy. Killed by a family friend, if I remember correctly. You have no friends here. If I were you, I wouldn't get into the habit of antagonizing your enemies. There may not be enough room in the family plot." He turns and storms out of my office, slamming the door behind him.

I lean back and grin. The reaction was exactly what I expected...and what I wanted. Now, Castillo's the one rattled. All I have to do is sit back and wait for the time to strike.

BYRON

I drop my shoulder and throw it into Derek's chest. He flies backward and slides across the polished court floor with a bewildered look on his face.

"What the hell was that, Byron?"

I drive the ball to the hoop. It drops through the net, and I come down on my feet next to where Derek is sprawled.

Dammit.

I scrub my right palm over my face to wipe off the sweat then extend my left hand to him. "Shit, I'm sorry, man. I got a little too aggressive there."

He clasps my hand and lets me pull him from the floor with a grunt. His soft blue eyes narrow on me, and he sets his jaw. "You've been like this all game. What the hell?"

He's right.

Our Saturday morning fun league has not been so fun today. It's been more of an outlet for my aggression and frustration over the whole situation with Steele than a playful game with buddies like it usually is.

Fuck. Luca, not Steele.

I can't stop thinking about it, though, no matter how hard I try. Even days after his appearance at the club and the revelation of who he really is, his dark eyes still haunt me day and night.

It's not fair to the guys to keep playing when I'm a liability on the court. Someone could get hurt because I'm in a shit mood.

"Let's just call it, guys." I raise my hands in apology.

A rumble of agreement comes from the other players standing around, watching my conversation with Derek, and I jog off the court toward the locker rooms before anyone can say anything else or question me about what just happened. I'm not sure I could explain it or even want to try.

Derek follows closely behind me, his heavy footsteps thudding against the tile floor in the locker room. "Are you okay? I mean, I know we really get competitive during the game sometimes, but you were taking it to a whole new level today."

I drop onto the bench in front of the row of lockers and pull my sweat-soaked shirt over my head. "Not really."

He sits across from me and bends down to untie his shoes. "What's going on? Something at work?"

Ha. I wish it were so simple.

There's very little drama at the club. Gabe and Savage ensure that by running a tight fucking ship...and by relying on me to keep things and people in line.

I shrug and shake my head. "Sort of. You remember me telling you about that guy I met a couple weeks ago?"

He glances up with a grin. "Yeah, Steele, right?"

Thank God Derek and I have never let our history get in the way of us being friends and being able to discuss shit like this. It can be so awkward with someone you've been intimate with, but we've remained close even though things fizzled out sexually between us.

At the time I told Derek about my night with Steele, I had no idea who he was or what a clusterfuck it would create.

I sigh and wait for him to look back up at me again. "Well, that's just it. He wasn't who he said he was."

His light eyebrows dip down low, and his eyes narrow on me. "What do you mean?"

I run my hand through my damp hair, then lean forward so no one else in the locker room can hear me. "It was Luca Abello."

He recoils. "Holy shit, man, as in the *Dom Abello* Abellos?"

I nod and shift on the hard bench. "Yeah, his son."

"I didn't even know he had one."

"I knew he existed—vaguely. But he left New Orleans like twenty years ago, and no one has seen or heard from him since, so I had no reason to think about it or suspect anything."

There's no way *anyone* could have anticipated his reappearance, especially like that.

Derek nods and reaches for his gym bag in the locker behind him. "How did you find out?"

I give a mirthless laugh. "After he got done stalking Storm, he came into the club for a meeting with the Hawkes and saw me there."

He jerks back to face me. "Do you think it was intentional?

Like a setup? Did he know who you were when he approached you that night?"

Isn't that the ultimate question?

It's certainly the one that's been rattling around in my head since he set foot in the club and I realized what a horrible mistake I had made.

I shrug and reach down to untie my laces. "I don't know. I can't help but think so. But I honestly don't remember what, if anything, he asked me about them or what information he may have tried to glean."

Derek pulls off his dirty shirt and tosses it into his bag. "What are you gonna do? Have you told the Hawkes?"

The man sitting across from me knows what the Hawkes mean to me. They're the closest thing I have to family anymore. He knows what they did for me, how they took me into their fold and treated me like one of their own from day one and put their trust in me. Derek knows everything. So, he understands what this means—for them and for me.

I could lose them forever.

I pull on a clean shirt and shake my head. "I don't know. I haven't told them. I just found out a couple days ago. I have no idea what to do." So much has happened since the last time I saw Derek at our last game. "Things have been all over the place there. The same day he had the meeting, Storm's house was burned down by this psycho chick."

His eyes widen. "Damn. That family sure goes through a lot of shit, don't they?"

There's a fucking understatement if I've ever heard one.

The Hawkes have suffered more than any one family should ever have to.

I laugh and shake my head. "Yeah, they kinda do."

"But you're gonna tell them, right?" He pulls on a clean shirt and raises an eyebrow, waiting for my answer.

Tell them what?

About the way he kissed me. About the way he touched me. About the way he fucked me...

My chest tightens at the same time my skin heats and my heart races with the memories.

"I have to." I just need to figure out how.

3

BYRON

This might've been a bad idea. Actually, bad isn't even the right word. Horrific. But now that I'm standing outside Steele's hotel room door, turning around and going home without confronting him doesn't seem like an option.

I need to know if what happened between us was a setup. If it was all some sinister plan to get information he could use on the Hawkes. Because it sure as hell didn't feel like it to me.

It felt real.

Real attraction.

Real sex.

But he may just be a really fucking good actor. Or I may just have been so desperate that I wasn't paying attention to the signs that should've told me something was very wrong with the situation.

Either way, it's my fault for not seeing through the act.

My heart thunders against my ribs as I raise my hand and rap on the door. It opens almost immediately, and Steele—no, *Luca*—leans against the door with a sly grin on his face in perfectly tailored black slacks and a white dress shirt with the top two buttons undone.

"I was wondering how long you were going to stand out here, debating whether to knock or not."

Fucker.

Of course, he knew I was here. Just one more situation where he has all the facts and I have zero.

I scowl at him. "We need to talk."

He nods slowly, and his onyx eyes trail up and down my body, undressing me just the way his hands once did. "We do. Come in." He motions backward into the room and holds open the door.

I brush past him, my shoulder making contact with his chest. That same jolt of electricity zips through me that did the night we met. His room is unchanged except the liquor bottles are a lot emptier than they were when I was here last.

He nods toward them. "You want a drink?"

I could probably use one, but maybe I shouldn't. It's essential to keep my wits about me when in the same room with this man. His scent permeates the air, and my cock hardens at the memory of being enfolded in him. Adding liquor to the mix would only make things worse.

Shit.

I scrub my hands over my face as he pours something into two glasses and turns back to me. He hands one to me and holds up his glass to clink it.

He can't be serious.

He raises a dark eyebrow. "Now, are you going to be rude?"

I scowl and clink my glass against his before I take a swig of the mystery booze, against my better judgment. The deep, smoky flavor of burnt peat hits my palate.

Jesus, he really does have good taste in alcohol.

I look over his shoulder at the bar and spot the 25-year

Laphroaig. He just poured me a hundred dollar shot like it was nothing.

Christ, this guy has more money than sense.

"So, what is it you want to discuss, Byron."

"I think you know, Steele, or should I call you Luca?"

He grins and drops into the seat across from me. "You can call me whatever you want. They're both my name."

"How is Steele your name?"

One corner of his mouth tips up as he stares into his drink. "I've never told anyone this story, and people have been asking for years, but for you..."

I roll my eyes. "Gee, thanks, I feel so special."

He chuckles. "Right after we moved from New Orleans to New Jersey, I got into a fight on the playground. The other boy kicked me in the nuts, and I barely flinched."

I cringe and reach down to adjust my balls just thinking about it. "How the fuck did you manage that?"

A shot like that would have most men—or young boys even— doubled-over on the ground and possibly vomiting.

He shrugs and takes a sip. "I don't know. His foot landed slightly off to the side. It hurt, but it wasn't as excruciating or overwhelming as everybody makes it out to be. I guess I was just lucky. Anyway, someone said I had balls of steel, and it kind of stuck. I added an *e* to the end of it because I thought it was cooler and would look more like a name that way when I was a kid."

I laugh and drop my head back. "Well, you definitely have balls of steel. The way you waltzed into town pretending to be somebody else then showed up at the club like that."

"I wasn't pretending to be somebody else."

Sure. Right.

And I'm a fucking virgin.

"Was it a setup?" I return my gaze to his because the only way to even hope of getting a read on Luca Abello is to be eye to eye with the man. "Did you know who I was when you walked into that bar?"

He takes a sip of his drink, but his eyes remain locked with mine over the rim of the glass. "What do you think?"

I would love to believe that what happened between us was genuine. Even if both of us only intended for it to be one night, I still don't want to think he only did it to gain information. I also don't want to admit to him how much it hurts to think that it was a setup. "Honestly, I don't know. All I do know is, I don't trust you."

"Who does these days?" He says it so casually, I almost feel sorry for him.

This is a man without friends. A man who likely doesn't have anyone he can truly trust in this world. I can't imagine what that would be like at this age. Mom and Dad may have deserted me when I came out, but I'll always have the Hawkes and everyone at the club who have become more of a family to me than my blood ever was.

In Luca's business, he doesn't have the benefit of being able to trust people the way I can.

I take a sip of Scotch and let the warm burn down my throat distract me from watching the way his muscles bunch and flex under his crisp shirt every time he moves his arm to take a sip or to shift his position.

Christ, I am in so much trouble with this guy.

Reason doesn't exist in the same world as Luca Abello.

He sighs and leans forward to rest his elbows on his knees. "I don't know what you want me to say, Byron."

"I want you to tell me the truth. Is that really asking too much?"

LUCA

It's asking more than he could possibly know. When I heard something outside the door and looked out the peephole, my heart began racing. I held my breath, waiting for him to knock.

I wanted him here, more than I care to admit. More than I care to examine now with him sitting here in front of me.

Those types of internal explorations only lead to disastrous truths.

I'm not one to respond physically to someone the way I do this man. Thudding heart, sweaty palms, cock half-hard the moment I saw Byron in the hallway.

It's a completely unexpected reaction. A dangerous one. For both of us.

He was a fling. A one-night stand.

The same thing I've done dozens of times with dozens of men over the last decade. Yet, the desire to see him again and the reaction when he actually showed up have me questioning my sanity.

I must be insane to even be considering this.

There's no room in my life for a relationship. There's no place for feelings or needing someone. It's not an option. Yet here I am, feelings things. Needing things. For him. From him.

Telling him about the Steele name and what I'm about to confess now are more than I've opened up to anyone in two decades. It's something I've never ever considered before— sharing my deepest, darkest truths and desires. Exposing myself so completely to another human being. It's contradictory to everything I've ever seen or been told to do.

Abellos cut themselves off. Build walls around themselves to prevent any potential weaknesses from penetrating. My crew in Jersey was the same. It's a way of life I long-ago accepted as an unfortunate truth. And being gay only made it more essential.

Yet, here I am, about to open my fucking mouth again because I don't want Byron to agonize over this.

I take another drink and lean back in the chair to watch him. He deserves the truth, whether I want to accept that or not. He's suffering, and the truth may put him at ease, at least a tiny bit.

"I had no idea who you were when I walked into that bar. I had been following Storm to make sure she was okay and to try to get a feel for how the Hawkes might react to my return, but I hadn't come into the club or seen you. At least, not up close. It was completely random that we happened to end up in the same bar, and I'm being one-hundred percent honest about that."

He narrows his eyes and studies me. The corner of his mouth droops slightly into a frown. I want to kiss that scowl right off his lips. Remove that distress and replace it with gasps and cries of pleasure. But he wouldn't accept that from me right now. The downturn of his lips says everything.

He doesn't believe me, and why should he? I'm the son of a mobster. I'm a mobster myself. I can't be trusted. I shouldn't be trusted. Even *I* wouldn't trust me if the positions were reversed.

The man who has occupied my fantasies for the last several weeks rakes a hand through his dark hair. He takes another sip of his drink and then sets it on the small table to his left. "When did you realize who I was?"

I can't help the smile that spreads across my lips. "I think it was when I was just about to stick my dick into you."

Byron growls, and I fight the pull of another smile. Seeing him rattled is a fucking aphrodisiac that seeps into my veins.

"You mentioned you needed to work the next day, and I asked you where. You said The Hawkeye Club."

Those words almost gave me pause that night.

Almost.

I was too far gone and too damn determined to get inside Byron to stop just because of the complication it would create.

He freezes at my reference to what we did—no doubt having the same memories race through his head that have been haunting me since that night—and covers his face with his hands. "Do you have any idea the kind of position you put me in?"

The laughter bubbles up uncontrolled, and I tilt my head to the side, picturing everything we did together. "Shit. I'm pretty sure I had you in half a dozen positions."

Maybe more...

Byron snarls at me and shoves up to his feet, his fists clenched at his sides. His jaw tics, and his nostrils flare. "You think this is funny? Those people are my family. My friends. And you're their goddamn enemy. This is not a fucking joke. My life is not a joke."

I set down my drink and hold up my hands as I rise. "I'm sorry. I wasn't laughing at you. I don't think you're a joke. I don't think this is a joke. I just couldn't help picturing how you looked that night."

How damn good you looked and tasted and felt...

Just as good as he looks right now. So fucking hot in his anger and frustration. It fuels his passion—passion I'd rather have focused on me in a totally different way.

I close the distance between us quickly and take his face in my hand before he can move away. He tries to pull back, but I hold him in place, forcing him to look me in the eye. "You've been thinking about it, too. Don't lie to me and say you haven't." I press my lips to his, not giving him any room for question about what I want.

Him. This. Now.

He stiffens for a second as he no doubt contemplates giving into his baser needs over what his head might be telling him. The internal struggle only takes a second before he sags against me and wraps his arms around my waist to drag me against him fully and return the kiss.

His hardening cock presses against me, and mine twitches. He may not want to admit he needs this, but his body and lips don't lie.

Fuck yes.

4

BYRON

I want to tell Luca no. I want to tell him to get his hands and mouth off me. I want to tell him this is wrong and we can't. I want to tell him I hate him because I should. I want to tell him all those things.

But I don't.

Because I can't.

I'm fucking putty in this man's hands. The heady scent that's all Luca—a mix of leather and Scotch—engulfs me. I return the kiss with the same fervent need he has. He presses his body against me—all hard and lean and desperate. My cock strains between us, and one of his hands slinks down and cups my crotch. He squeezes harshly and growls against my lips.

"This. This is what I want." His words aren't a request. They're a demand.

And I'm not going to tell him no. This is what I want, too. No matter how much I tried to deny it. No matter how much I've fought it since I found out who he was.

When it comes right down to the heart of it, he is what I want. I haven't needed anyone or anything as much in my entire life as I need this man right now. Even as I thought about him since learning the truth, there was something else mixed with the anger. Something far more powerful that's now overflowing between us. Unadulterated desire.

Everything else can wait. Everything else can be ignored.

My frantic hands tug at the buttons of his shirt. They finally cooperate, and I shove the crisp material off his shoulders, exposing his chiseled, tanned chest and arms. He releases his hold on me long enough to let his shirt fall to the floor. Then his hands slide my jacket off and pull at the hem of my T-shirt, and he tugs it up and over my head. His lips meet mine again, hungry for the same thing.

I unbutton my jeans and jerk the zipper down as he unbuckles his belt. Every movement of his hands has me craving his touch. This is happening at breakneck speed, but it feels more like slow-motion, like the world has frozen around us.

He wraps his arms around me and walks me backward until my knees hit the bed. I tumble onto the mattress, and he comes with me and presses his hard body against mine.

The weight of him on top of me heats my skin as memories of our night together come roaring back. He growls in my ear and nips along my neck and collarbone.

Stop. Stop.

It's what I should be saying, but I don't.

I can't.

Not when his tongue flicks across my nipple, and then he sucks it into his mouth.

"Oh, fuck." The words tumble from my lips in a gasp.

Yes. Yes. Yes. Who ever thought making bad decisions could feel so fucking good?

His hands work to shove my pants to my knees, letting my

cock spring free while he continues his sensuous assault on my pecs. A large, rough hand wraps around the base of my dick.

Sweet fuck.

I almost come on the spot. I bite my cheek, groan, and shift my hips up into his grip. He moans against my flesh and strokes my shaft with a tight hand. His thumb brushes across the head, spreading the bead of pre-cum over it.

"Jesus fuck."

He hums in response and continues to torture my nipples when all I want is his hot mouth wrapped around the place his hand now controls.

Christ, I can't take it anymore.

I bury my hands in his hair and push, urging him down. His eyes flick up to meet mine. The heat blazing in their dark depths sends fire dancing over my skin. He kisses his way down my stomach and engulfs my shaft in one smooth motion.

The wet heat of his mouth has me gasping and digging my hands into his hair. "Fuck, Luca."

He swallows me even deeper, and the head of my dick rubs against the slick back of his throat. I fight the tingle at the base of my spine.

Shit. I can't come this fast...

But with his tongue sliding along my shaft and the way his lips suction around me...I won't last.

I roll my hips and thrust. He moans around me, and a growl rumbles low in his chest. The vibration along my cock is my undoing.

"Fuck!" I shoot my load straight down his throat as he digs his fingers into my hips and sucks like a fucking wild man.

And he is one. When we're together, he's completely unbridled, out of control yet controlling everything at the same time.

"Jesus Christ." I gasp and suck in a breath as my entire body shakes and tingles.

He sucks my dick hard one more time and releases it with a satisfied grin. "Now I finally know what you taste like."

After we met at the bar, it was fast, dirty, and straight to business. I spent time on my knees for him, but when it came to reciprocating, it was clear he planned to get me off in other ways that night. And he did. More fucking times than I can count. Having his mouth on me now was literally a fucking dream come true.

Luca rises to his feet and shoves his pants all the way down. His massive erection springs free, and he strokes it once, twice, then kicks off his pants and drops his knee onto the bed between my legs. He leans down, stopping with his lips a hairsbreadth from mine. "Fucking fantastic."

He presses his lips to mine and demands entrance. I open for him, and the salty taste of my release on his tongue has me hardening again.

Fuck.

Those dark eyes flare as he backs away and pulls my pants from my feet. He tosses them over his shoulder without caring where they land. My cock throbs. Hard seems to be my only state whenever I'm around him, and it slowly thickens again, watching him tower over me.

He steps between my legs and slaps the outside of my thigh. "Turn over. Up on your knees."

God...yes.

I roll onto my stomach and push myself up onto my hands and knees. I look over at him. He strokes his length as his dark eyes rake over me. His free hand reaches out and squeezes my butt cheek, then he smacks it hard as he moves between my legs and presses his cock against my hole.

The man who is my worst nightmare and greatest dream all rolled into one leans over me and pushes his chest to my back. His hands come down on top of mine, and his warm breath flutters against my ear. He nips at it and growls. "I've been dreaming about fucking this ass for weeks. I hope you're ready."

LUCA

I grasp Byron's firm cheeks and spread them open. My cock aches, and I rub it between them. He moans and shifts back, offering himself to me.

Like I would turn him down.

Even if I wanted to, at this point, he's unleashed the beast in me, the part of me that stops at nothing to get what I want. It's what makes me great at my job, and no one has ever complained in the bedroom before.

Certainly not Byron...

I smack his cheek hard, and he rocks forward but comes right back to me. A pale red handprint forms, and I brush my fingers across it lightly, sending a shudder through him. It shouldn't make my chest swell with pride the way my touch affects him, but it does. And getting inside him again will be absofuckinglutely mind-blowing.

I press my thumb against his opening and push in. He groans and tightens around it.

Fuck.

This is what I've been fantasizing about. His total surrender. Even though he fears me. Fears who and what I am. He's still giving himself to me.

I growl and smack his ass with my other hand. It's so good with him. Every fucking moment we spent together that first night was more memorable than anyone else I've ever been with. It's *him* I dream about, *him* I picture when I stroke myself.

Only him.

I probe at him, preparing him for what is going to be some fucking rough sex. As badly as I want Byron and don't want to hurt him, especially with the taste of his cum still on my tongue, this won't be slow or gentle. I don't do it any other way.

The drawer to the bedside table glides open easily, and I grab the bottle of lube and drizzle it over my dick and where my thumb is buried inside him. I grasp my dick and press the head at his opening as I pull out my thumb. He groans and drops onto his forearms, pushing himself up at a different angle. I enter him slowly and clench my jaw against the desire to shove into him in one hard stroke. His hands tighten on the bedspread as I push deeper. With every inch that slips inside him, I grit my teeth harder.

So damn close.

Having his cock down my throat almost had me blowing my load five minutes ago, but I needed this. I want to be inside him when I come. I want him to feel it, to know what he does to me drives me fucking insane and makes me think and do things that are dangerous for us both.

I finally push in to the hilt. He groans, and I lean down over him and press my chest against his back. I wrap my hand around his throat and tilt his head back until his eyes meet mine. "You feel fucking incredible. You like having my cock inside you?"

He grunts and tightens his muscles around me. I growl and press my lips to his. Our tongues duel as we fight for control. He brings up an arm and tugs at my hair, angling my head the way he wants it.

I withdraw my hips slightly and push back in. He moans into my mouth and rolls his hips. I growl and nip at him before I pull my chest away.

No more playing around.

I reach around and grasp his hard cock.

"Fuck!" He glances over his shoulder, and I flash him a grin as I dig the fingers of my other hand into his hip and shove inside of him.

He gasps as I start a driving rhythm and stroke his cock in time with my thrusts. His hips move as he pushes into my hand and meets my strokes.

"Christ, I'm gonna come again." His strangled words make my dick throb inside him, and I increase my pace, driving into him and stroking him with an end in sight.

It hits me without warning. I plunge deep, and the orgasm slams into me. I clutch onto his hip and squeeze his shaft as I blast my load. He grunts, and his dick hardens in my hand as he comes with me.

I release his cock and wrap my arm around his waist to pull him back against me. He sags into me, and I turn and drop back onto the bed, dragging him along. He pulls away and rolls off to my side, away from the evidence of his orgasm.

My chest heaves, and the air of the room chills my sweat-slicked skin. I run my fingers down his spine, and he shivers. "Byron?"

He lifts his head and turns it to look at me. I grin at him, but there's no humor in his eyes. None at all. The dark brown appears almost black in the dim light of the room, and any softness that may have existed there only moments ago has been replaced by something else.

He's already letting his guilt and loyalty to the Hawkes weasel its way into his head. He can't even let himself enjoy a few brief moments of post-orgasmic bliss without second-guessing the decision to give into me again.

The man is as infuriating as he is irresistible.

I push myself up onto my elbow and narrow my eyes. "Don't do that."

"Do what?" He rolls to the side of the bed and drops his feet to the floor, giving his back to me.

Oh, hell no.

I grab his shoulder and turn him back to face me. "Don't let your loyalty to them ruin *this*." I motion between us. "*This* is good. Very good. Don't pretend it's not just because *they* wouldn't like it."

He pulls away from me and rises to his feet. "You don't get it."

I do get it, but nothing I can say will change his mind. Actions speak louder than words, though. I climb off the bed and step right up to him until I can feel his chest thudding against my own. I slam my lips against his and grab his cock.

It's all that needs to be *said*.

5

BYRON

The walk of shame isn't anything new for me. Since my move to New Orleans, I haven't exactly been careful or particular about my partners, and it's made for some awkward morning-afters. Far more than I care to remember.

But today has to be the worst.

By a fucking longshot.

Acid churns in my stomach as I pull on my jacket and zip it. I tug my hood around my face and take one glance back at Luca's sleeping form. His chiseled chest rises and falls rhythmically, and his perfect lips part slightly as he releases a little groan in his sleep. The disheveled dark hair I had my hands buried in last night makes him look even more dangerous than when every strand is perfectly in place.

The smell of sex hangs in the air, mingling with the leather-and-spice scent that's all him.

Shit.

It has my cock hardening again. As if a half dozen orgasms weren't enough over the last twelve hours. If I don't get the hell out of here, I'm going to continue this self-destruction well into the afternoon.

I slip from his room and out into the hallway. It's deserted, and I release a sigh of relief and slowly close the door until it clicks shut behind me. I freeze and listen for sounds that it woke Luca, but welcomed silence greets me. I managed to get away without a confrontation, and it's still early enough there hopefully won't be very many people up to witness this.

God willing.

Though the man upstairs hasn't really done me many favors. Crap childhood. Shitty parents. The one good thing I have that I've always considered to have been divine intervention, the Hawkes, is now threatened. There's no way my relationship with them will survive my affair with Luca.

It can't.

I drop my head and hit the back staircase that will let me out into the side alley, away from the main lobby and the most likely place for prying eyes. My boots pound on the metal stairs, the sound reverberating down the stairwell and through my ears.

It's a welcome reprieve from the voice in my head.

I've never felt so dirty in my entire life, and that's saying a lot considering the things that were said and done to me back home.

It's not easy being a gay kid in Utah. Especially back then. Even though I wasn't out yet, people knew. People gossiped. People whispered. People did a lot worse. People were not kind. Which is how a skinny, quiet kid ended up in New Orleans, spending his time in the gym bulking up so he could protect himself. And I can now. If anyone throws a punch or tries anything, I'm confident I can defend myself or anyone else who needs it.

But what I can't protect myself from is Luca. That arrogant man, with his flashy suits and confident smile, is enough to drive me fucking mad.

I shove out into the alley and inhale the fresh morning air.

The salty tang of the water mingles with bacon and something sweet trickling from a propped-open door down the alley—probably the kitchen of the hotel.

My stomach rumbles, but I can't eat. It would just sit like a damn rock in my gut with all the guilt that's slowly destroying me from the inside out. I jog down the block to my car with my head down. Looking anyone in the eye is impossible after what I did with Luca, after what I let him do to me.

Last night was supposed to be about confronting him. Learning the truth about that night we spent together. Getting information about what his plans were for the Hawkes. Instead, I caved to his charms and demands and practically fucking begged him to fuck me.

Way to go, Byron. Slut.

The man has some sort of weird hold over me. It makes me forget why this is so wrong...until the light of the morning when I see the face of every Hawke and the way they stare back at me when I tell them what I've done.

Judgment in their eyes.

The hurt.

The betrayal.

They've suffered enough of that for ten lifetimes.

Now, I'm going to be the one who does it again.

And I will do it because I know I'll be back here...with him.

Maybe not tonight, maybe not tomorrow, but I won't be able to stay away from Luca, and that fucking sucks.

I climb into the car and crank the ignition. Music blares from my stereo. "Blame It On The Night..."

Jesus.

I let out a mirthless laugh and shake my head as I throw the car into drive. The words of the song pour through the car as I pull out of the parking spot and make my way toward home. Each and every lyric slices at my heart and has guilt clawing at my chest.

Fuck this song.

It couldn't be any more accurate for my life right now.

I would love to have something else to blame but myself. Maybe some sick twist of fate or karma getting back at me for some old action. Or even better, blame it on booze last night and the night we met. But I was stone-cold sober last night—at least, I was when he kissed me—so I can't blame it on alcohol, as much as I truly wish I could.

It was a decision I made with my dick instead of my head. The kind of decision I knew I would be regretting just like I am this morning, but I did it anyway because I'm weak. Because that man's dark eyes and thick black hair and rippling, rock-hard muscles, that man's kiss, that man's laugh, that man's everything drive me absolutely fucking insane and make me forget about anyone or anything else when we're in the same room.

He's an addiction I can't afford, but one I know I won't break anytime soon.

Only a fucking moron would get into bed with Luca Abello again, but I did.

And I will.

LUCA

Alessandro sticks his head into my office. "Mr. Abello? Sir?"

"What?" I stare at the spreadsheet on my screen, trying to make sense of the numbers.

Why the hell is he interrupting me now?

"We have a problem."

I sigh and turn away from my computer. "What's that?"

He walks in and stands behind the chairs across from my desk. I motion for him to sit. He's one of the few holdovers from when Dom was still around. The rest have either scattered or moved on to other areas of work. As long as they're not with one of my competitors, though, I don't care.

I reward loyalty, but a man needs to be able to support his family, and with the Abello empire in ruin, some didn't have a choice but to get out of the business.

"What's going on?"

He shifts nervously and motions behind him, toward the front of the building. "I've noticed a car sitting down the road the last couple days."

I snort.

Jesus, this guy is not very observant.

"Just one car?"

He nods.

"And just the last couple of days?"

He nods again, slower this time, almost as if he's anticipating what's coming. But he's not smart enough for that. He probably just caught the hard tone of my repeated question.

"You really suck at your job, Alessandro. I've been followed since the day I met with the Hawkes. They rotate cars and who is watching me to try to remain inconspicuous, and I've had to ditch them several times already."

His dark brows furrow. "Really?"

I sigh and relax back in my chair. "Yes, really."

This guy is a dolt.

No wonder Dom never trusted him with anything more important than being the muscle.

"What is it I pay you for, exactly? If you didn't know this was happening, how are you supposed to protect me and the business?"

He shrugs. "I-I-I don't know what you expect, sir."

Jesus.

I scrub my hand over my face. "Get out of here." I wave him out.

"What are we gonna do about it?"

We aren't doing anything.

I scowl at him. I would love to walk right up to the car and tell them I know they've been following me and to back the fuck off, but I don't have much to hide. Other than going from here to the hotel and to dinner or meetings, nothing I do for the business is hidden or really matters in the grand scheme of things if people were to find out. Anything dirty I have my hands in is well-hidden behind dozens of layers of protection—drugs, guns, girls, they're all practically invisible. I'm as clean as a whistle where the business is concerned.

My personal life, however...

It's exactly why I haven't gone back to The Back Pocket or any other bar when I needed to release some tension. That, and there was only one man I wanted to help me in that area.

Last night with Byron only refreshed and enforced that the man has everything—intelligence, passion, determination, loyalty. He cut straight to my heart and kept my cock hard from the moment he walked through that door until he snuck away this morning.

These feelings. That need. It's very dangerous in this world.

It's one of the reasons Mom and I were sent back to Jersey all those years ago. The man who never wanted me around knew what my lifestyle meant for him, what his enemies would do with the information if it ever came out.

It's just too dangerous to have something you care about so close, and while being sent away had everything to do with protecting himself, not Mom or me, he had the right idea.

I can't let myself care about Byron, and I can't let myself feel bad for the guilt he holds for lying to the Hawkes about what we've done. I can't let myself care about his history, about who he is or where he came from. I can't let myself care about any of that because even if this were a world where he could be safe, if I were a man he could be safe with, once he tells the Hawkes, it will be over anyway.

There's only one person I can ever care about. I grab my phone and dial the number.

"Luca, I wasn't expecting to hear from you today. Are you okay?"

"I'm fine, Mom."

She sighs. The same sigh she's given me a thousand times over the years. The sigh that elicits that little bit of guilt about leaving her behind to come back to New Orleans.

"You can always come down here, Ma." I hated leaving her there, but she isn't alone. Not really.

She has her cousins and friends, her church group, and the Italian society meetings. She has a life there, one that she's built over the years since putting NOLA in her rearview.

"You know I can't." Her words are barely audible, but the heavy emotion in them screams loud and clear over the line.

She's right.

I can never go back there, and she can't come here. There's too much bad blood. The people of New Orleans are not going to welcome her with open arms after what *he* did. After what I'm continuing to do.

She may not know what I'm up to, even though she no doubt suspects it, but what *he* did will haunt her for the rest of her life.

How could it not?

She tried to bury her head in the sand when they were married. She tried to ignore what was happening around her, but she definitely knew. And every time his name appeared in the paper, anytime any scandal arose, anytime there was any danger and it might have touched us, it was like another stab to her poor heart.

Getting out of NOLA was the best thing that ever happened to her...and me.

"You can always come home, baby."

An ache forms in my stomach with her words.

Home.

I don't even know what that word means anymore. Is NOLA my home? After being kicked out? Is Jersey my home just because Mom is there? Even if I wanted to go back, it's out of the question.

"No, Mom. I can't." I burned all my bridges there the day that they found out what I am. There's no going back. I'm staying in New Orleans. This is my *home*, for better or for worse. This is where I started, and it's where I will end. Hopefully, sometime far out in the future and with less of a *bang* than dear ol' Dad got.

She sighs again, and a momentary silence hangs on the line. I know that silence. She's gearing up for a question she knows I probably don't want to answer. "Have you reconnected with the Hawkes yet?"

It's a loaded question, one she knows the importance of, but I knew she would ask. She knew one of my major goals in returning home was to regain my friendship with the people we both once considered family.

I run my hand back through my hair. "It's complicated."

Which she knows.

It almost broke her when she heard what happened to Ben and the truth about Stone and his relationship with Dom. There are so many things she feels guilty about, but allowing Dom to get his hooks into Stone at such a young age is toward the top of that list. She feels like she let it happen because she agreed to leave with me. That somehow, had we stayed, Stone wouldn't have been dragged so fully into that world.

She doesn't understand the reality. There was no staying. If she had fought going to Jersey, he would have made sure we went there, or somewhere else, by force, if necessary.

"I'm sure it is, honey. If you talk to them again, send my love."

A genuine feeling from one of the most loving people I've ever met. Despite everything, Mom always tried to protect me and shield me from the harsh realities of who I am and what the world is like today. It's not her fault she failed miserably at it. And she truly loves the Hawkes and misses them as much as I do.

"I will. I love you, Mom."

"I love you, too, baby. You're sure you're okay?"

This time, I sigh. *Okay.* It's such a simple word but such an incredibly difficult concept. "As okay as I can be. Goodbye, Mom."

I end the call and lean back in my chair. My eyes sweep over the office. Nothing has changed since Dom sat here. Except for the chair my ass is in. This is where he ran his empire. This is where he ordered horrible things against innocent people. This is where he died.

I won't repeat his mistakes.

I can't.

6

LUCA

"Mr. Abello? Sir, there's someone here to see you."

Who the fuck is bothering me now?

It's been one thing after another ever since I got here, but now that I'm no longer spending my time keeping an eye on Storm and have been in the office more, it just means even more bullshit. In the week since Alessandro noticed the car, things have piled up and gotten even more complicated. I haven't even tried to contact Byron again, even though my finger has hovered over my phone a hundred times wanting to.

He needs to come to me when he's good and ready. Forcing him to make a decision now would only back him into a corner, and a man like Byron backed into a corner would only result in him lashing out at someone. Mainly me. I'm the one he sees as the enemy, not the Hawkes. He can't see that what he's doing by giving in to what he thinks *they* will accept and condone is completely backward.

Time will change that.

In the meantime, I'm stuck here dealing with months of

ignored businesses and partners and a thick-headed moron for a bodyguard.

"Who is it?"

Alessandro clears his throat and looks down the hallway toward the front door. "Pretty sure he's the chief of police."

Shit.

"Okay, show him in."

I should've known this would happen eventually. I can't come into town and set up shop and not expect to draw attention. Attention from the very people who were trying to nail the former Abello don for years before he was killed.

A silver-haired man in his fifties enters my office, and I rise to my feet. "Chief O'Donnell, is it?"

Alessandro closes the door as I walk around the desk to shake the man's hand. He knows I don't need him in here protecting me. I'm more than capable and willing to do what it takes with my own two hands, if necessary.

The chief takes my hand and grips it tightly. "Yes, Daniel O'Donnell, Mr. Abello."

I flash him a smile. "Please, call me Luca."

His hand drops from mine, and he shakes his head. "I'm not sure I'm comfortable with that, Mr. Abello."

Wouldn't want anyone to think you're too friendly with the bad guys.

I suppress a chuckle as I return to my seat with a shrug. "Whatever you're comfortable with. So, what can I help you with today?"

He lowers himself slowly into one of the chairs across from me, and any humor or friendliness that was on his face a moment ago instantly dissipates. "Well. Mr. Abello, here's where we stand. I've heard rumors over the last couple months of you being around, but I only recently got confirmation that you've reestablished your father's business dealings."

I chuckle. "Let me guess, a little birdie named Gabe told you."

The corners of his mouth turn up. "Yes, a little birdie told me, though I'm not sure why you think Mr. Anderson has anything to do with this."

He's lying.

It was Gabe, and it's not surprising. Given that Gabe single-handedly took out the former Abello boss and at least half a dozen of his best men on more than one occasion, his relationship with the chief of police, especially when it comes to my family, is quite strong. He probably made a call to the chief the moment I left the club the other night to let him know I was back and what I was up to.

"So, you thought that required a personal visit?" I raise an eyebrow. I have to give the man credit; he doesn't even flinch under my stare.

"As you know, your father's, let's just say, 'activities' caused a lot of people, myself included, a lot of grief, and I wanted to make sure we weren't going to be having any similar problems now that you're here."

I steeple my hands in front of my mouth and sigh. "I don't have any intention of causing any trouble, sir. I'm here to hopefully clean up the Abello name."

He snorts. "Do you *really* expect me to believe that you decided to go legit and squeaky clean? I know what you did in Jersey, so don't play innocent with me. You're here because there's a power vacuum that was created when your father was killed, and there are other players like Castillo who tried to swoop in and snatch up some of your territory and business, but nobody has really dominated yet. This is your opportunity to step in, so let's not play games."

I raise my hands. "I don't play games, but you can't expect me to divulge business secrets and plans to you."

He chuckles and rises to his feet, smoothing his button-down shirt. "No, I don't, Mr. Abello, but what I do expect is for you to not cause any fucking trouble. I went through a lot with your father for a long time, and he managed to slip through our fingers, but I won't let that happen again if you start up with the same bullshit." He moves to the door and turns back to me. "You saw how easy it was for Gabe to take your father out, and while I don't condone indiscriminate killing or vigilante justice, let's just say, if you start causing any problems, I won't be sad to see you go the same way your father did."

Wow. This chief has balls.

I like him.

I rise to my feet and walk around to shake his hand again. "I appreciate the visit, Chief. I'll keep what you said in mind."

"I'm sure you will." He smirks as he opens the door and steps out in the hallway.

Alessandro nods at him, and I hook my thumb toward the front door to let him know the chief is free to go. Anything else wouldn't do any good at this point. He's a good man just doing his job while I'm a bad one just trying to do mine. I'm not going to interfere with him, as long as he doesn't interfere with me.

BYRON

The words on the page in front of me all blur together into a giant mass of black against the white background. Nothing registers, and nothing has in the hour I've been staring at this book. The one I've been dying to read. The one I was so engrossed in before I met a certain dark-haired man with eyes the color of night.

People chatter around me, and the clink of silverware and mugs fills my ears, yet none of it distracts me, helps clear my mind, or manages to make me forget the sound of his voice or his words.

He wasn't wrong. About what he said.

I'm an adult and should be able to be with whoever I want without guilt.

I shouldn't have to ask for permission or look to anyone for any sort of confirmation that I'm doing the right thing. It's not anyone's business.

Then why does my gut hurt so much when I think of what's going on with him?

Relationships should make you happy. Content. Fulfilled. You shouldn't be agonizing and worrying constantly. But this is a unique situation and is very different than any other man I could be with. This is about as complicated as it gets.

"Byron?"

I jerk up my head at the soft, familiar voice. Nora stands next to my table, looking down with concern etched onto her beautiful face, her slim, pale eyebrow raised over a shrewd blue gaze.

"Are you all right?"

Not really.

I force a smile. "Yeah, I'm fine. Are you okay?"

She rubs her huge belly and holds up a Styrofoam cup. "Decaf tea. I sure miss my caffeine, but even though they say it's safe in small doses, even one cup makes this little one jittery, and he kicks me relentlessly."

I chuckle. "You're due soon, right?"

"Yeah, just a couple weeks."

I can't believe how fast time has flown. It seems like only yesterday she was applying at The Hawkeye Club and Dani stormed in to try to rip her off that pole.

"Are you anxious to be done?"

She points to the empty chair across from me. "Mind if I sit?"

"No, of course not."

Maybe some company will help take my mind off all this.

She settles in across from me and drops her purse onto the table. "I don't know. This whole pregnancy thing is kinda weird."

I snort and take a sip of my luke-warm coffee. "Yeah, I bet."

"So, what's going on with you? You definitely don't look like you're okay. You look like you were a million miles away, staring off into space."

I really can't tell her what's going on. Not as wrapped up in the situation as she is.

Keep it vague.

"Have you ever been with someone you know is really bad for you?"

She snorts and takes a sip of her tea. "I don't know that it's that simple." She twists the cup in her hands and gets a faraway look in her eyes. "There are probably people who think me being with Stone is bad for me. Given everything that's happened and all the history that exists between us..." Her gaze flicks up to meet mine. "Does this guy treat you badly?"

I shake my head. "No, actually, he treats me really well."

Luca may be aggressive and demanding, but he's never been abusive or cruel. He just knows what he wants and takes it. And he's anything but a selfish lover. He takes care of me the same way I do him. And then some.

"Did he cheat on you?"

I shake my head again. "Not that I know of, but it's not like we've discussed being exclusive, either, so even if he has been with somebody else, I really can't fault him for that."

She raises an eyebrow at me over the rim of her cup. "Then what's the problem? Why do you think he's bad for you?"

And here's where things get tricky.

"It's not so much what I think; it's what I know. He's not the type of guy I should be with, and there's a history that makes things even more complicated."

Her eyes narrow on me. "A history that makes things even more complicated?" She releases a sigh and sets her cup on the table. "Look, Byron, you know I'm not one to dole out advice. I'm usually the one looking for it, but if you want to talk about complicated histories, I don't think you get much more complicated than Stone and me. We were hot and hard and heavy for only a short period of time before the revelation about Stone killing my father came out, and I wanted nothing to do with him." She laughs and rubs her belly. "Then I found out I was pregnant, and he came back, and everything changed. Not because of the pregnancy, but because I'd had time to really think about the situation and grow up a little bit."

The truth of what Stone did had a devastating effect on all the Hawkes, but what it did to Nora and Dani was ten-fold. I can't even imagine learning someone so close was responsible for the death of your parent, even if it wasn't done maliciously.

She shakes her head. "I'd be lying if I said Dani and I don't still struggle sometimes with the truth of what happened, but what these months taught us is that we all do things in a split-second that can have a ripple effect of consequences we never expect. Stone was just a boy. He was protecting the man who was like a father to him. There's nothing more to it than that. My dad was just in the wrong place at the wrong time with the wrong people, and I've learned to accept that. If I can get over the fact that Stone killed my father, still love him, and still be planning a future and having a child with him, then whatever it is that's in the history between you and this guy can't be that bad."

Well, damn.

When she lays it out like that, it does make it seem a little less complicated. Except it's not my history. It's theirs. And just like Stone was responsible for Dani and Nora's father's death, Luca's father is responsible for Ben and Caleb's.

And while the sins of the father should not necessarily be taken out on the son, Luca isn't exactly doing anything that's helping to convince everyone he's not going down his father's path. He's still a mobster with bad intentions.

I nod and offer Nora a tight smile. "You're right, and if it were about my own past, I might agree with you. But this involves other people, other people important to me."

She narrows those shrewd eyes again, and I can practically see the wheels turning in her head. She glances at her watch. "Crap, I have class in twenty minutes. I have to go, but just think about what I said. Life is too short to get hung up on what other people want or to bend to what other people think about your relationships. If he makes you happy, if he treats you well, if you can see yourself having a future with him, then it doesn't really matter what anyone else thinks or feels about the guy."

Words of wisdom from a mere babe.

"Thanks, Nora."

She grins at me.

"I miss having you around. When you were at the club, you always managed to brighten my day."

She chuckles as she slowly lumbers to her feet. "There are days I miss it, too, but I don't think that this," she rubs her belly, "would be popular with the clientele."

I laugh. "You'd be surprised. Some people have some real freaky fetishes."

And I seem to be a masochist to actually be considering trying to make this work with Luca.

7

BYRON

L uca's strong arm wraps around my waist. I squeeze it gently and then roll away from him to sit on the edge of the bed. My feet hit the carpet, and I focus on the slit of sunlight streaming in through the sides of the curtains on the floor-to-ceiling wall of windows.

Shit.

I hadn't intended to stay this long. I hadn't intended to come at all last night, yet when I left the club, I found myself driving the familiar route here instead of the one home. I rub my eyes, and he shifts behind me.

"Where are you going?" His deep, gravelly voice, heavy with sex and contentment, envelops me.

Anywhere but here.

Every time we're together, the guilt intensifies. It's like having a ten-pound elephant sitting on my chest, restricting my ability to breathe. The longer this goes on, the longer I lie to myself and to my friends, the worse it becomes.

Today, it's unbearable. Almost a living thing with its own pulsing heartbeat and presence.

"Stay." His large warm hand lands against my naked back, and his finger lazily strokes down my spine.

A shiver rolls through me. It's not from the chill in the air. "Don't." The word comes out as a harsh command, not a request. I glance at the clock. "I have to be at work in like five hours, and I need to shower and get cleaned up before I go."

There's no way I can concentrate at the club with Luca's scent on my skin. I don't even want to get into my clothes with him all over me.

"I'm gonna take a shower."

It's a stall tactic. A way to avoid any sort of intimate talk without running out like my tail is on fire.

I rise to my feet and glance down at him as I walk around the bed toward the bathroom. He reclines against the pillows with his arms tucked behind his head, making his biceps bulge out in such a fucking sexy way, my cock stirs to life. *Again.*

His eyes scan my body, and a grin spreads across his lips as he focuses between my legs. "Come back to bed. We can dirty you up some more before you take a shower."

Of that, I have no doubt.

One thing I can't deny is Luca's ability to take me to another plane of existence when we're together.

"Can't do it."

Won't do it.

Not today. Maybe not again. If I can ever find the will to say no to him for good instead of crawling back.

I haven't managed it yet, though. My head and my heart war so often at this point, it's practically World War III going on in my body. And it feels like both sides are losing.

"Why not?" He raises a dark brow. The sparkling pools of molten sex that are his eyes try to drown me.

"You know why not."

The humor in his gaze disappears in a split-second, replaced by something that looks a hell of a lot like disappointment.

Why? Because he's not going to get laid again or because there's still so much between us that makes this impossible to maintain?

He watches me where I stand at the end of the bed, but he doesn't say anything. He doesn't lecture me or try to start another argument about why us being together isn't a giant slap in the face to the Hawkes like I believe it to be.

We've had that conversation more times than I care to count in the weeks this has been going on. It's almost become a ritual. Show up. Fuck. Argue. Fuck. Slip away while he sleeps.

Real fucking healthy.

But this time, he just lets me go to the bathroom without another word.

I let the door shut behind me and crank the water on as hot as it goes.

Right now, the surface of the sun wouldn't be enough to scald away the feeling of his touch across my skin, his cock driving into me, his lips pressing against every inch of my exposed body.

Jesus.

My cock is at full attention by the time I step into the shower. I let the cascading water burn my skin, trying to wash away the memories and the guilt. But they won't disappear, and the traitor between my legs throbs and begs for my touch until it's almost excruciating.

I could try to fight it. Turn the water to ice cold to try to shock it from my system. But I'm too weak, broken, and beaten down by the man who should—given his reputation—treat me like shit, but instead, acts like he can't get enough of me and only wants me to be free from what weighs me down. So rather than ignore my aching dick, I reach down and take it in my hand with an angry groan.

I don't want this. I don't want to want him. I don't want to need him.

Yet, lately, it feels an awful lot like I do need him. I need his touch. I need his caress. I need his assurances that everything is going to work out because I am so fucking terrified of losing my job and my friends that some days, my heart is racing so fast, I feel like it might explode.

Luca's the only thing that occupies my mind as I stroke my length hard and fast. The water won't wash away the pain as much as I want it to. The pain of knowing that he's becoming so important to me that I might just risk everything for this.

The orgasm hits me hard, and I grit my teeth as I shoot streams of cum against the tile of the shower. Tile that probably cost more than I can even process, and I just came all over it thinking about Luca, the man who should be my enemy. The man who is ten feet away from me in a massive bed. The man who has worked his way into my heart.

I really am a mess.

And that man is only making me messier.

LUCA

Byron is going to be pissed when he gets out of the shower and sees what I've done, but he didn't leave me much choice. As soon as I saw that look on his face when he sat at the edge of the bed, I knew he was going to leave. He was going to run away from this, away from us, away from what he's feeling, and that's the last thing I want right now.

The last few weeks have been nothing short of eye-opening. Everything I thought I knew about my business, everything I thought I knew about myself, it all flew out the window as soon as I met Byron and let him work his way into my life.

This business will always be important. It's why I came to

NOLA in the first place. It's why I've always closed myself off to the possibility of any sort of a partner or relationship.

But what about happiness? What about what makes my heart race and makes me feel alive?

Right now, it's not business. It's not the idea of cleaning up the Abello name. It's not the money or the power. It's being here, like this, with Byron.

I don't know how it happened, but I somehow went from a dedicated bachelor for life to making underhanded moves to keep this man in my bed. I need him to keep coming back. I need him to stop running. I just fucking need him.

When the end of the day rolls around, and all the stress and frustration of trying to run and rebuild a crumbled empire has mounted, all I want is to come here and be wrapped up in that man. So much so, I even risked going to his place when he didn't show up here the other night. Even knowing I'm being followed, I couldn't stay away.

So, what I did may not be ethical or right, and God knows he's going to be angry, but it's necessary to get what I want. What I need. I don't like taking no for an answer. Not from employees. Not from enemies. Not from anyone. I've given Byron time to sort through his reservations about our situation. Time to make a decision. But he hasn't. It's time to talk, whether he wants to or not.

The bathroom door opens, and I turn from where I stand at the bar. The sound of his bare feet padding across the floor toward the bed have my cock hardening.

"Luca? Where are my clothes?"

I pour myself a Scotch and turn around to face him. "Would you like a drink?"

He stands with wet hair, droplets of water still sprinkled across his chest, and a towel wrapped around his waist. "No, I want my clothes, so I can go home and get ready for work."

I set down my drink and pour him one. "Well, that's going to be difficult because I sent them to the laundry to be cleaned. They won't be back for at least two hours, or maybe more, depending on how busy they are."

Anger flashes in his eyes. "Why the fuck would you do that?"

To keep you here.

I shrug and walk over to him with his drink in my hand. I hold it out, and he glances down at it like it's a grenade instead of twenty-year aged Scotch. Now is the time for honesty. There's no point in trying to hide why I did it.

"Because I knew you were going to leave, and I wanted to spend some more time with you. Deal with it."

"Deal with it?" His eyes darken, and he clenches his fists at his sides. "That's all you have to say?"

"What else is there to say?"

"You arrogant prick—"

I hold up my free hand. "Now, now, there's no need to name call." I shove the glass into his hand and move back to retrieve mine from the bar. "Have your drink. I ordered food from room service."

He growls.

I glance over my shoulder at him. "And don't look so distressed. Is spending time with me really all that bad?" I raise an eyebrow. "You haven't objected to my company the last several weeks and have practically torn my clothes off when you got here. Your cock was already rock hard for me the moment I opened the door. Don't pretend otherwise."

Byron glowers at me and stalks over to drop down into one of the chairs on the far side of the room. Anger rolls off him in waves powerful enough to feel them even with all this space between us.

I lean back against the bar, completely unabashed in my nakedness. "Why are you so scared of staying here and hanging out with me?"

Every time we're together, it's the same. Byron tries to rush out with some excuse of needing to work or slips out while I'm still asleep to avoid confrontation.

He takes a swig of his Scotch and runs his hand through his wet hair. "You know why."

"Do I?"

"Don't play stupid. It doesn't suit you."

I chuckle and shrug. "I don't know why you're so angry. Why don't you tell me because I'm honestly clueless over here?"

Byron has done his best to keep me at arm's length emotionally even when he wants me physically close and gives in to me every moment we're together. I know what I would like to think he was going to say, but I need to hear it from his mouth, from his lips.

He needs to say it. Not just for my benefit, but for his own. Until he voices it, it won't be true for him, in his head or in his heart. I know what it's like to pretend something doesn't exist, that it's not a reality. I lived a fake life. So, while I can sympathize with what he's going through, I'm not going to enable him or it to continue.

He drops his head and stares into his drink. "If I sit here and talk to you, if we have any more deep, meaningful conversations, if I'm in the room with you without us fucking, I'm going to have to admit that I care. And I'm just not fucking ready to do that."

8

BYRON

That confession hurt more than the beating I took senior year of high school before I learned to defend myself, before I bulked up, before I learned not to start fights but to know how to end them.

I've been fighting against admitting it to him, let alone myself. So, the words burned leaving my lips more than the Scotch in my hand does going down.

A tiny smile tugs at the corner of Luca's lips, and he takes a sip of his drink while maintaining his nonchalant pose, leaning against the bar stark naked.

It's what he wanted. It's what he was trying to get me to say.

Arrogant prick.

Luca is a manipulator, through and through, and he always gets what he wants. If that's me, then it's fucking hopeless to even resist him. I'm learning that very fast.

"Was that so hard, Byron?"

I jerk to my feet and storm across the room to stand just inches from him, so close that the heat of his body radiates against my cool, naked skin. "It was that hard, and you fucking know it. Why are we playing these games?"

"Because you wouldn't tell me the truth. You wouldn't tell me how you feel. You've been running away from me every chance you get, only to come running right back."

"I think it was you who was running to me the other night."

When he showed up unannounced at my doorstep earlier this week, part of me was terrified he knew where I live, but the bigger part was just so damn happy to see him that I literally ripped the buttons off his shirt trying to get him naked.

It wasn't my finest moment. Yet, knowing he had come to *me* instead of me rushing to *him* gave me a sense of power I never thought I'd have with Luca. Rushing him out the door as soon we were both sated wasn't exactly the "adult" thing to do and isn't something I'm proud of even now, but having him in my domain, leaving his scent and presence and memories all over every-thing...it would just make it that much harder when this finally ends.

He tilts his glass toward me. "Touché. But here's the difference between you and me, Byron. I've been nothing but open and honest with you about everything."

I snort-laugh at him and take a slug of my drink. "Except your fucking name."

"I never lied to you about my name. That's a version of my name."

I scowl at him. He reaches back and sets his drink on the counter behind him then takes mine and sets it next to his. His hand finds my hip where the towel is wrapped, and his thumb brushes along that hypersensitive hipbone, sending a shudder through my body and hardening my cock almost instantly.

His eyes drift down to the tent in the towel. "I'll say it again; let's not pretend. Very soon, you're going to have to make a deci-sion about whether you trust me. And until you do, you'll keep coming back for more, just like I will with you. Because I haven't felt like this about anyone, well, pretty much ever."

His words choke the breath in my throat.

Ever?

Luca raises his hand and brushes his thumb over my lips. "I've never had the opportunity to be who I really am, to be with who I want, to do what I want to do. It's never been an option in my life. So maybe this is all just lust, maybe this is all just because there's an opportunity for more than a one-night stand, and I want to take it, but it doesn't feel that way to me. It doesn't feel that easy. And nothing that's good is ever easy, which makes me all that more confident that this is just as good for you as it is for me."

The back of his other hand brushes against my now fully hard cock, and I groan and lean in to him.

A knock at the door has me jerking back. "Shit."

He grins and leans in to press a hard, brutal kiss against my lips. "Food is here. How unfortunate, I was just getting ready to indulge in something else."

Jesus, he has a filthy mouth.

One I now can't stop picturing wrapped around my dick.

Fuck.

He brushes his shoulder against mine as he passes on his way to the door. No doubt intentionally.

Is he going to answer naked?

He pauses to grab a robe from the closet and ties the sash before he tugs open the door.

"Mr. Abello, I have your room service order."

Luca nods, but when the man tries to step through the door pushing the small cart, Luca holds up a hand to stop him. "I'll take the cart, thank you."

"You don't want me to come and set it up for you?"

"It's not necessary. Have a good night."

The man disappears, and the door closes. Luca didn't want

him to come in and see me. It shouldn't be surprising. People know who he is here. It would be a huge scandal if there were a half-naked man in his room at three in the morning. That has me rubbing at the tightness in my chest as I go sit at the dining room table in the corner. He talks a big game about wanting this to continue, yet he keeps it hidden.

He pushes the cart toward me and then lifts the lids off the two plates. "Steak frites. I hope you're hungry."

I hadn't realized I was until I stare at the food and my mouth waters.

The fact that he played such a dirty trick to get me to stay pisses me off, but my stomach tells me to let it go for the moment. It's not like I have many other choices in this unless I want to leave here in a towel.

LUCA

The anger still lingers in Byron's bourbon eyes, but he seems to have come to some sort of acceptance since the food arrived. Watching Byron wrap his lips around the piece of steak and the tiny little moan he gives has me shifting uncomfortably.

Too bad the food didn't arrive ten minutes later.

"So, Byron, you've hinted at your past, but I'm curious how you ended up working for the Hawkes."

He pauses for a moment and chews his steak, probably wondering what my ulterior motive is for asking, but there is none. I really just want to know about him and the people I came home to try to mend things with.

Byron swallows and assesses me a moment longer before finally sucking in a deep breath. "I'm from Salt Lake City. It isn't one of the friendliest places to grow up when you're gay. I didn't officially come out until I graduated from high school, but people knew. I was scrawny and nerdy and not into sports or any of the other things that might have helped me mask who I am."

My chest aches at his confession. I did have those things. Boxing, football, other "activities" that weren't so legal. Even women. They were all things I used to hide what I was. Once Mom and I were sent away, it was made very clear to me that I couldn't be open about what I wanted and still hope to survive in the world I was born into.

Byron pops a fry into his mouth, then continues. "My parents are very religious, and when they found out their son was gay," he shrugs, and pain crinkles the corners of his eyes, "they kicked me out."

Jesus.

He takes another bite and chews slowly, and I do the same. I thought what happened to me was rough—sending Mom and me away so that he wouldn't have to be seen with me, let anyone have anyone know his son was gay—but it sounds like what Byron went through was a hundred times worse. At least we had financial support and other family to go home to.

"I came to New Orleans because I had a friend I had met through a youth program one summer who lives here. He let me sleep on his couch, and the first thing I did was start working out," he snorts in feigned laughter, "like hard-core working out. I had been beaten up too many times in high school, and I didn't know how to defend myself, so I lifted. I took boxing lessons. I did whatever I could to make sure it would never happen again."

My fists clench around the fork and knife in my hands. The very real desire to fly to Salt Lake City and track down every single human being who ever touched Byron courses through my blood. I barely suppress a growl, but I don't want to stop his story, so I stick a bite of steak into my mouth and chew.

I may still go to SLC.

Byron shrugs. "I also looked for a job. I worked at a few gas stations, a couple fast food joints, and then one day, I drove past the Hawkeye Club." He pushes his food around on the plate. "It kind of struck me that one of the easiest ways to blend in and for people not to question my sexuality was to work at a strip club."

"Did it really matter anymore if people knew you were gay?" I raise my eyebrow at him.

He pops a couple French fries into his mouth and considers my question. "It did to me then. It mattered far longer than I care to admit."

I can't say I know what that feels like. I've never had the option or opportunity to *not care* about what people think. The second we set foot in Jersey, even at ten, I knew what was expected of me, and up until the incident in Baltimore, I managed to hide my true self from the world and the people who would do me harm.

"I get it. You had been hurt, emotionally and physically."

He silently nods and meets my eyes. "I think what happened back home with my parents just put me in a mindset of my business is not anybody else's and that it was too much of a risk to let people know."

I chuckle at that because he has no idea what risk really is. The kind of risk I faced when "friends" in Jersey found out. The gun that was placed to my temple. The words that were said. The promises made. But he struggled and suffered, just the same. It was simply in a different way.

"So, you just walked in there and asked for a job?"

He chuckles, and the first hint of humor flashes in his dark eyes. "Pretty much. Savage and Gabe were still really young back then, and the club had only been open for six months. They were still struggling to find good staff, and I swore to them I was reliable and would never miss a day at work. They hired me to bartend even though I had no fucking clue what I was doing, but I learned fast, and within six months, they made me the manager."

"That's a lot of trust to give someone so quickly."

His body stiffens.

Poor choice of words? Or exactly the right ones to get to the heart of everything that's happening between us.

He nods slowly. "And I always appreciated them doing that for me."

I set my silverware down and lean forward to rest my elbows on the table. "And that's why what we're doing is killing you so much? Because you feel like you're betraying that trust?"

Anger darkens his eyes. "Aren't I?"

A pain slices at my stomach.

How can he not see?

"No. You're an adult who is perfectly capable of and has a right to make his own decisions, especially about who to be romantically involved with. You've had enough people with an opinion about who you fuck. Are you going to let the Hawkes control that now?"

He glares at me, and his fingers tighten so hard on his fork that his knuckles go white. "They're not controlling anything."

"Aren't they? Because it seems to me like you're refusing to give this an actual chance because of them."

He scoffs. "An actual chance? I don't even know what to do with that." His silverware clatters to the plate, and he shoves away from the table and paces the room. "I don't know what to do with any of this."

I motion toward the seat he just vacated. "You can start by coming back over here and sitting down and finishing your meal. Go from there."

9

LUCA

Saint and Caroline stare back at me dumbstruck. Neither one of them expected the revelation that just came out. The fact I'm not hiding I'm gay from them seems to have thrown them completely.

I can see why. If the roles were reversed and I were meeting with a powerful and dangerous crime boss, and he told me, I would suspect a trap.

It's a big secret, one they could use against me in any number of ways. But if I'm going to demand Byron face his feelings for me, I would be a fucking hypocrite if I didn't come clean with Caroline when she came here and put her life at risk to try to help her friends. *My* friends. The very people I'm trying so damn hard to find my way back to.

If Caroline or Saint choose to reveal this information in a way that hurts me, I'll deal with the consequences. Until then, there's only one way to move.

Forward.

"Now, is there anything else you wanted to discuss today? I'm a very busy man and have several appointments later to attend."

She pulls her lip between her teeth and glances at Saint nervously before returning her focus to me. "Well, there is one more thing. I'm hoping to ask you for a favor."

I chuckle and lean back in my chair. "You have some balls, Ms. Brooks. You came here, trying to blackmail me with information you didn't even have, and then, when I give you exactly what you're looking for you, you ask me for a favor?"

She forces a tight smile. Saint growls deep in his chest. The big man looks ready to leap across the desk at me, but he won't. He has a role to play, and it isn't the instigator. Savage and Gabe would never hire him if he didn't know how to handle himself in a situation like this, and he's not dumb. The intelligence in his eyes as he stares me down is more than clear.

Caroline glances at him and sighs. "Look, I'll be honest, my reason for coming here was twofold. I had hoped to get you to back off the Hawkes to make sure we'll all be safe. But I've also been looking for a big story to do for the newspaper, something that might help me move up the ranks. I thought an exposé on the new crime boss in town might be just the ticket." She holds up a hand. "However, I'm not going to out you. That's just...too low. My ethics wouldn't ever permit me to do that anyone, even you. So, what if I flip the story?"

I raise an eyebrow at her.

Where is she going with this?

I didn't think she would out me. She knows how dangerous that would be for her, and for me, even though I haven't directly threatened them, yet *flipping* the story is intriguing.

"How do you mean, Ms. Brooks?"

She leans forward in her chair, and her eyes light up. "Well, what if instead of an exposé, we did a series of interviews. We present you as a businessman here to take over some of the legitimate businesses your father had and to clean up the Abello name."

Saint snorts. "So, you lie?"

I chuckle. "Now, now, Saint, I made it very clear during my meeting with the Hawkes that's exactly what I'm here to do. Am I still going to dabble in my father's businesses that are not so legal? Of course, but I'm not my father, and what happened under Dom Abello will not happen under Luca Abello. I want to have a clean image here, so the story might be just what I'm looking for."

Caroline's eyes light up. "Really?"

Most men in my line of work try their damnedest to stay out of the spotlight. They may lead extravagant lifestyles, but when it comes down to it, talking with reporters and being in the newspaper and on television only hurts them. But I'm not like the other men in this business.

"I think it's a wonderful idea, Ms. Brooks, and I'd be happy to sit for as many interviews as you need to complete your story. Why don't we start next week?"

She grins, and Saint scowls even harder. I rise and walk around the desk. I hold out my hand to her.

Her tiny palm meets mine. "Thank you, Mr. Abello."

"Please, call me Luca."

She giggles awkwardly. "Luca."

Saint rises to his feet and towers over even me. The man is just massive. There's no other way to describe him. I hold out my hand to him. He pauses for a moment, staring down at it before his dark eyes find mine. He clenches his jaw and reaches out to shake with me. His massive meat hook practically crushes my fingers. He's making a statement. I get it loud and clear. If I harm a hair on Caroline's head, he's going to kill me.

And I have no doubt he would. He would find a way. No matter how much security I have, no matter how much I do to try to protect myself, Saint would make it happen.

But I have no intention of harming this woman. Not only would the Hawkes never forgive me, but Byron would never set foot in the same room with me. There's no reason to make Caroline and Saint enemies any more than they already are. I have enough enemies.

What I don't have are friends. And while we may never go out for drinks or dinner together, we may never celebrate a holiday and snap photos, what we can do is enter into a mutually beneficial agreement. One where she gets what she wants for her job, and I get what I want to help cement my presence here in NOLA.

A very public profile story would shove it in the face of anyone considering stepping up to me that I am here to stay.

She could be exactly what I'm looking for.

BYRON

I jerk awake and rub my eyes to clear away the sleep. I push myself up in bed and glance around the dark room.

What the hell was that?

Bam. Bam. Bam.

Who the hell is pounding at my door at two a.m.?

I throw back the covers and make my way through my dark apartment to the door.

Bam. Bam. Bam.

Getting woken up in the middle of the night by some asshole is the last thing I need. I finally managed to fall asleep after battling with myself for hours about wanting to go to Luca's. For once, common sense won, and I didn't go crawling over here.

I glance through the peephole.

Shit. What the hell is he doing here?

The smart thing to do would be not answer. But he won't go away if I don't. I scrub my hands over my face, unlock the door, and tug it open. Luca shoves past me, turns around, and pushes the door closed. The lock clicks into place.

"What the hell, Luca?"

His dark eyes roam over my nearly naked body, and he takes a step forward, closing the distance between us and backing me into the door. His left hand hits the wood, followed by his right, caging me in against it.

My heart flutters, and my cock hardens, and he hasn't even touched me.

I finally manage to find words. "You can't be here."

There isn't enough will-power left in my body to have him this close. Not tonight. Maybe not ever.

He shifts his hips forward and presses his erection against mine. "I came to tell you something important."

I shove my hips back against his, trying to put a little distance between us, but all it does is cause a delicious friction that has me biting back a groan. "I don't think you coming here to tell me you need to get off is important."

A sly grin curls the corner of his mouth, and he brushes his thumb over my quivering lip. "That wasn't what I came for."

The desire burning in his gaze and the hard dick pressed against me says otherwise. He's a fucking liar. Always has been. Always will be.

"Then tell me whatever is so important and leave."

He leans in and brushes his lips against my ear. His warm breath floats across my skin, sending goosebumps skittering all over. "I had a lovely visit with some of your friends today."

I freeze, and when he pulls back, I narrow my eyes at him. "Who? What did you do?"

"The lovely Miss Caroline Brooks and her boyfriend, Saint Clarke."

"Shit."

He chuckles and shifts his hand up to press it against my naked chest. My heart thunders under his palm.

I swallow through a dry throat. "What did you do?"

He raises a dark eyebrow at me. "You have so little faith in me? That hurts. They showed up at my office of their own volition. Ms. Brooks is interested in writing a piece on me for the newspaper and Saint...well, he was interested in protecting Ms. Brooks."

I practically choke. "A story on you? What kind of story?"

That grin appears, the one that simultaneously makes my cock throb and my gut churn.

"The kind that could help establish me as a legitimate businessman a lot more quickly than if I tried to do it on my own."

"So, you agreed?"

He nods. His thumb brushes slowly across my nipple. It pebbles under the attention, and I bite back a groan.

"I did, after a rather lengthy conversation revealed some very intimate details of my life."

My blood runs cold as he rolls his hips against mine. I clench my fists at my sides. "You didn't."

He quirks an eyebrow. "So what if I did? You're going to have to tell them eventually, aren't you?"

I shove against his chest to get him to back away, but he doesn't move an inch. "What the hell did you tell them?"

"Oh, ye of little faith." Hurt touches his black eyes. "They know I'm gay. I needed to tell them to explain my departure from New Jersey. Ms. Brooks was digging around into an incident that occurred in Baltimore several months before I arrived here that was going to out me anyway."

I close my eyes and shake my head. "Jesus..."

This is so, so, so bad.

Even if he didn't tell them about *us*, Saint and Caroline knowing he's gay puts his life at risk. A life I care way too fucking much about.

"They won't say anything."

My eyes fly open. "How can you be so sure?"

"It wouldn't advance any goals for Ms. Brooks since I agreed to the interviews and story. And they know outing me would be a death sentence for them. And me. And if they knew about our involvement, you too."

Fuck. Fuck. Fuck.

The last thing I need is the Hawkes or anyone connected with them snooping around and talking to Luca. It would only take one wrong word, and they would know everything. They would know my betrayal.

Luca leans in and brushes his lips against my ear again. "Don't worry, Byron. They don't know about us."

I growl. "There is no us."

He grinds his cock against me again, and mine twitches in response. "I beg to differ. There is very much an us. You're just in denial."

His lips are on mine before I can retort. The kiss is hard and brutal, just like the man delivering it. His hand moves off the door and captures my face, holding me steady as he pushes me against the hard surface.

Fuck. Just fuck.

This. Us. It will destroy everything.

But I need it once more.

Just one more night to be selfish. One more night to enjoy the little bit of joy he brings me. The way he gets my heart thundering and my blood rushing in my ears. Even when he's being an arrogant bastard, I want him. Maybe even more.

I wrap my arms around his waist and turn him, so he's against the door, and I'm *finally* the one in control.

It doesn't happen much with us, but maybe it's what I need to close the door on this fucked-up chapter.

He groans against my mouth as I tug at his suit coat and shove it off to drop to the floor at our feet. I yank at his belt and zipper until his pants drop down to his knees. His tongue lashes at mine, greedily drinking in the thing I need just as much.

Ravenous hands claw the waistband of my boxers and shove them down while I do the same to his. I dig my hands into his hips and yank him away from the door. He opens his mouth to say something, but I shove him around to face the door and push him against it.

He looks over his shoulder, and his eyes flare—but not with anger. No. It's pure lust staring back at me. He's not going to fight me on this. He's going to let me take control.

And I won't waste time questioning why.

Because as soon as it's over, so are we.

10

BYRON

The silence of the club engulfs me.

It's always a bit odd to come into work early in the morning before it's open. Everything is so still, so quiet, so different than what it normally looks and sounds like. No bumping bass music. No naked women hanging from poles. No drunk men, hooting and hollering.

It's the only time of day I get to actually get work done—schedules, ordering, staff issues, it all takes time I don't have once we're open. But today, I'm not relishing the loneliness.

Being alone means thinking.

Thinking means regretting.

Regretting means guilt...and I've had enough of that already.

The past few weeks have been a whirlwind of incredible nights with Luca and mornings filled with early walks of shame, awkward goodbyes, and dark clouds of disgrace.

I knew I'd go back to him. It was as inevitable as the sun rising every morning and setting every evening. But every time I knocked on his hotel room door, I shoved all the reasons I shouldn't be there into a locked box in the back of my mind. I gave into my base needs and desires. Damn the consequences.

Pleasure like that can cloud a great many things. Like the truth. Being here, in the stillness of the club early in the morning, the reality slaps me right in the face.

I can't keep doing this.

The longer I put off telling the Hawkes, the worse the fallout will be. For all of us. I may have finally ended things with Luca that night at my place—after he let me fuck out all the hate and pain—but it doesn't absolve me of what happened, of what I did for weeks.

And every day I come here and look the Hawkes in the eye, I feel worse and worse.

I set my bag on the bar, pull out a stool, and open the morning paper. The to-go cup of coffee in my hand is still hot enough to scald my mouth as I take a sip. The burn is welcome. Sharp pain urging me to do what needs to be done. I need to tell them.

Soon.

I flip through the paper, mindlessly skimming the headlines to try to clear my head at least for a little while until I almost choke on my coffee.

The New Don in New Orleans
Luca Abello Speaks Out
Story Page 5

Shit. Shit. Shit. Shit.

I flip to page five.

He warned me this was coming eventually, but I wasn't ready for it. Not at all.

In the weeks since I finally broke things off with him, I tried to forget it all, tried to push things down and lock them away in some dark place I never need to revisit. Somehow, I thought that might let me get away with never telling the Hawkes.

It was over anyway, so why bother telling them at all? Because of *this*.

This is not good. This is not good at all.

The coffee I just drank and the protein bar I ate on the way here roil in my stomach as I dive into the article.

Everyone knows the name Abello and not for a good reason. Domenico Abello was the king of the New Orleans underworld. He ruled with an iron fist and a quick trigger finger and was responsible for a hurricane of carnage in the city over the last several decades. But there's a new Abello in town, one who wants to make it clear he's not his father. He's here to be Luca Abello, the son of Domenico, who left New Orleans at age ten and recently returned. He insists he's come back to the city of his birth to clean up the family name and to run his father's legitimate businesses.

If the apple can fall far from the tree, that certainly seems to have happened with the younger Abello. I've had several very pleasant sit-downs with him during which he explained his thought process about returning to a normal life in New Orleans, his and my home, for better or for worse.

"I left with my mother at age ten for many reasons, but mostly because she didn't want me around my father, and he didn't want me around him, either. I wasn't raised in his world and never had any interest in joining the family business. He was heartless. He was an unforgiving a**hole. Can I say that in this paper?"

I couldn't help but laugh along with him at that comment. Luca Abello is handsome and charming, and it's hard not to like him despite reservations about a man with the infamous last name...

My eyes glaze over as I read about him reopening the liquor distribution company, the waste management company, and a handful of other business ventures. All merely a cover for revamping his father's criminal empire.

Shit. Shit. Shit.

Did he say anything to her? Did he let anything slip?

Even if it's not printed in black on the page, that doesn't mean Caroline doesn't know and didn't tell everyone.

He was pissed when I ended things. I anticipated a blowup. A fight. Him raging and telling me he wasn't going to let me go. But I got the opposite. Hard, dark, stoicism was all he offered as he pulled his clothes on after I fucked him brutally. He cast one look over his shoulder at me before he closed the door on us.

It's what I wanted. It's what *I* did. But it still broke me more that Luca could so easily walk away than if he had put up some sort of a damn fight.

Maybe he didn't because he planned to use this article to get back at me, to hurt me in the worst way possible. By telling the Hawkes.

No.

If he did say something to Caroline and she told, I'd have been eaten alive by angry Hawkes descending on me by now. They don't know. *Yet.*

It's still too early for anyone else to be here. Savage and Gabe are probably still at the gym, and Saint and Caroline haven't been coming in until mid-morning.

Good.

I need time to think. Time to figure out a plan on how to approach what will undoubtedly be a very uncomfortable conversation. It's something I should have done long ago.

I set the article to the side and drop my face into my hands.

How did I manage to fuck things up so badly?

If I had just kept my dick in my pants, none of this would be happening. I wouldn't be fighting my attraction to the wrong man while hiding something so important from my best friends and employers.

I guess the Hawkes were right. When an Abello shows up, he only brings bad things with him.

LUCA

The click of my Zegna shoes against the concrete echoes through the warehouse. Walking the same path Dom did has a chill climbing up my spine. The last time an Abello set foot in here, he was only days away from getting gunned down by Gabe.

I wander over to a stack of pallets filled with six-packs of beer stacked so high it almost reaches the ceiling, and I turn back to Adam. The manager of the liquor distributor we've owned for years trails a few steps behind me.

"We all set?"

He nods, stops, and examines the clipboard in his hand. "Yep, we have pretty much everything back in stock, and we're ready to start deliveries again later today."

Excellent.

It's taken far too long to get things rolling again. Part of that is my fault, but a lot of the blame can be placed on the men Dom left behind, the ones who were too stupid to step up and take charge.

I glance at all the product filling the massive space. "And where do we stand there?"

Adam glances up at me and raises an eyebrow. "Uh?"

Good Lord, it's like talking to a wall sometimes.

"How have my father's former customers responded to us re-entering the market?"

His eyes widen. "Oh. Well," he rubs his jaw and averts eye contact, "we have about fifty percent of them back."

I must have misheard him. "Did you say only fifty percent?"

He nods.

Fuck.

My delay in getting down here after Dom's death has really fucked us over on a lot of fronts. Even people who were loyal customers have been forced to move on and find new distributors because the dumbasses who should have stepped up and been running his businesses had no idea what to do after he was gone.

I snarl and push past him. "Give me a list of everyone who bought from us before his death and everyone who has not returned as a customer. I will make personal visits to each location and speak with them."

There isn't time for this, but there's no other option at this point. I can't let things go to shit any more than they already have. The job is all I have left, and time is ticking away to cement my position.

He shakes his head. "You don't have to do that. The guys can just go over there and make sure they come back to us."

I scowl at him. "Are you an idiot? I'm talking about going over there and having a conversation with them. Explaining the situation so that they understand why it's beneficial for them to go with us."

Of course, this *stugots* just wanted to run over there and break some bones. That's how Dom would have done it. That's how my old partners in Jersey would have, too.

"Don't for a second think that you're going to get away with what happened under my father's regime. This is a new Abello crew. I'm the new face of the family, and I'm not going to create the same negative connotations with the name that my father did."

That would make my entire move here pointless.

I could have up and moved anywhere—as long as it wasn't Jersey. I could have gone somewhere no one knew me or my legacy. I could have chosen somewhere that being gay wouldn't have even been blinked at. But I didn't. I came here to reclaim my birthright and name.

"Listen to me carefully, Adam, and make sure the men understand this, too. There are much more subtle and polite ways to make the same point. And you're going to have to learn that if you want to continue to work for me." The threat in my words should be clear. People don't just walk away from the Abello crew. They disappear.

He gulps and nods slowly. "Okay, boss. I got it."

"Make sure the other men get it, too." Starting out with a cull could bring down negative publicity I don't need right now.

I shove past him on my way back toward my car. These idiots are going to make it impossible for me here. The Hawkes already think I'm nothing but a two-bit thug. And I'm fairly confident Byron believes it, too.

That's why he ended things. Even when he was coming to me, he was so cut off and so distant at times. I can only assume it's because of the Hawkes and because of what he thinks I am. And now that it's over, it looms over me like a dark cloud, threatening to unleash a torrent.

Violence is just part of the business and necessary at times, but it's not the starting point. It's the last resort. Live by the sword, and you'll die by it.

At least, that's the way the old saying goes. And in my experience, it's true. I've seen too many men go down with a bullet to the head or chest with their very own steel clutched in their hand. Some deserved it. Some didn't. Either way, they lost their lives because of how they chose to live them.

I can see why Dom's death was inevitable. You can't rule by violence and expect to walk away from it unscathed. Maybe I'm fucking stupid for thinking it's an option to be more diplomatic, but I can't bear to see innocent people harmed the way the Hawkes were.

Maybe I'm weak, or maybe I'm just more humane than he was.

Those weeks watching Storm and Angelina, seeing how disorganized and chaotic their lives had become, witnessing the hurt and the anger and the distress on Storm's face every day, and knowing Dom put it there was almost too much. But I forced myself to watch, to take note, because it's only through knowing the worst fallout that I'm learning where my lines are drawn.

I'm learning more and more that line blurs, but if I want to have any chance of gaining the Hawkes' and Byron's trust, I need to play it safe. If I ever want Byron to come back, he needs to see we can all coexist without hate and mistrust.

I need to be the good, bad guy, not the bad, bad guy.

A chuckle falls from my lips as I slip into the car.

The good, bad guy...is there even such a thing? Or is it just wishful thinking on my part to believe I can walk that tightrope without falling over into the abyss?

11

BYRON

I've never actually felt fear having to climb the stairs to go talk to Gabe or Savage about something before. This place has always felt like home. It's always been somewhere I felt safe and protected among friends. But one reckless decision and weeks of shitty ones after it has turned them into potential enemies or me one to them.

Even disappearing for a day to try to wrap my head around what to say to them hasn't helped. It's the first time I've ever missed a day from work, let alone without calling. Under normal circumstances, I'd be feeling guilty about it, but my guilt is all tied up at the moment.

I clutch Caroline's article in my hand and approach her open office door. Dani just left, so Caroline should be available.

From reading the article, it seems Caroline had a pleasant experience with Luca. That's not surprising. The man could charm a habit off a nun. If Caroline likes him, maybe she'll be on my side of this, a friendly face in what will surely be a sea of pissed-off people.

I knock on the jamb and summon every ounce of courage I have with a deep breath.

"Byron? Where have you been? Is everything okay?"

I hold up her article. "We need to talk."

She narrows her eyes on me but waves me in. "What's going on?"

Sex. Betrayal. The usual...

I stop in front of her desk and suck in a deep breath. "I need to have a meeting with Savage, Gabe, and Saint to tell them something, and I'm really hoping you'll come in and support me."

Her eyebrow wings up. "Support you how?"

I tuck the article under my arm and brace my hands against the chair back. My head drops down. I can't look at her when I say this. "I need to tell them I've been sleeping with Luca Abello."

"Holy shit."

I snap my head up and meet her wide eyes.

Her mouth opens and closes a few times before she manages to get some words out. "Are you serious?"

I wish I weren't.

I press my lips together and nod.

"For how long?"

My hand shakes as I run it through my hair. "The first time was well before we knew who he was. I swear I didn't know who he was. I didn't realize until he came to meet with everyone here that the man I knew as Steele was actually Luca."

"Holy hell. Do you know how huge this is?"

I growl lowly. "Of course, I do. Why do you think I'm dreading it so much?"

She holds up her hands. "Okay, okay. Sorry, of course, I'll go with you for moral support."

And undoubtedly to witness the fireworks.

She rises from her desk and walks around. I follow her out the door and down to Saint's office with my heart in my throat.

This is it. No going back now.

Saint flashes a grin when he sees Caroline. "Everything okay?"

She nods backward toward me standing behind her. "We all need to go have a meeting with Gabe and Savage right now."

His dark eyes narrow on us. "Why? What's going on?"

She holds up a small hand. "Just trust me, it's better if we do this all at once."

He sighs and rises from his chair. "Okay, Bambi." He presses a kiss to her forehead before following us down the hallway to Savage's office. Gabe and Savage's voices float out into the hallway. Saint stops at the jamb. "Hey, guys, you got a minute?"

They both look over toward the door. "Yeah, what's up?"

He steps inside and allows Caroline and me to enter. "Caroline and Byron need to talk to us about something."

Savage sighs and leans back. "While I'm glad you've surfaced again, Byron, why do I have a feeling I'm not gonna like this?"

Gabe examines us as we enter. Caroline takes the chair next to him, and Saint sits on the edge of Savage's desk.

I move to the other side of the room where everyone can see me and hold up the newspaper article. "We need to talk about Luca."

Gabe's pale eyebrows rise, and his eyes flick between Saint and Savage. "What about him?"

I've gone over how I was going to tell them a thousand different times, yet in my head, all I see is a massive wall of nothing.

How do you tell your friends that you betrayed them? How do you tell them you're literally sleeping with the enemy?

I guess you just come right out and say it. "I've been sleeping with Luca."

"What?" All three men yell the word at the same time, all with wide, hard eyes.

Gabe glowers. "You're joking, right?"

I shake my head. "I wish I could tell you I was."

Savage scowls. "How the hell did this happen? I didn't even know he was gay."

A sigh slips from my lips, and I twist the article between my hands. "It wasn't long before we knew he was in town. He told me his name was Steele. I didn't find out who he was until he showed up here to meet with you guys."

"Jesus Christ." Savage's eyes flick over to Saint. "Did you know about this?"

He crosses his massive arms over his chest. "Of course, not. You think you wouldn't know if I knew?"

Savage's eyes narrow on Caroline. "Did you know?"

She scoffs. "No. I mean, I knew Luca was gay, and so did Saint, but not that he was sleeping with Byron."

Savage tosses Saint a dirty look then returns his attention to Caroline. "You knew he was gay? How?"

She shrugs nonchalantly. "I found some things when I was researching him for my story. He admitted it to me, but I told him I wasn't going to out him."

Savage scowls at Saint and fists his hands on his desk. "And you knew about this?"

He nods. "Yes."

"Why didn't either of you tell me?" Savage's deep voice is even harder than usual, the thin edge of control about to break.

This is what I've been dreading. The blowup. The explosion of rage from the head of the Hawke family.

Caroline raises her eyebrows. "Why would I? It's totally irrelevant to your situation with him, or I thought it was, until..." She waves at me. "Really, how the hell was I supposed to know Byron was boinking the guy?"

Boinking? Really?

Everyone chuckles a little bit, and it breaks some of the tension building in the room.

Did she do that on purpose?

I clear my throat. "Look, guys, this is obviously a very difficult situation for all of us. I don't want you guys to think I betrayed you. I didn't know who he was when I met him."

Savage narrows his eyes at me. "When you met him..."

He didn't miss that. He doesn't miss much. He may have been able to forgive the first night when I didn't know. When I couldn't have known. But when he knows I kept returning once the truth was unveiled, a nuclear bomb will detonate.

"But you continued to see him when you knew who he was, and you didn't tell us?"

I nod.

His blue eyes go ice cold. "Are you still seeing him?"

I shake my head. "No. I told him I couldn't see him anymore. I just couldn't deal with the sneaking around, the not being able to trust him, not being able to trust myself..."

Savage opens and clenches his fists several times while silence fills the room. So much has changed since the first time I sat in here with him, begging for a job and for him to trust me. We've gained so much and lost so much just the same. Now I'm begging for forgiveness and trust again, only this time, I don't deserve it.

Finally, Savage shakes his head and sighs. "A year or two ago, I probably would have exploded at you and fired you on the spot for this kind of betrayal." His eyes shift over to his best friend, and a knowing look passes between Gabe and him. "But I've learned something over the last few years. Sometimes we do things for love, or lust, that we wouldn't do otherwise. Things that others may see as unforgivable." He turns his gaze on me. "I almost lost Gabe because of his relationship with Skye. For something so stupid and petty. I'd love to think I've grown from that and can sit here and say I understand why you were with him."

I shake my head. "I'm not asking you to understand. It doesn't matter anyway, like I said, it's over."

He considers me for a moment. "Good. I'm glad it is, but my primary concern is where *we* all stand."

Gabe rises and moves over to stand in front of me. He reaches out and places large hands on my biceps. "Byron, we've trusted you with our business and our lives for years. You're a member of this family. We believe you when you say you didn't know who he was, but the fact that you kept this from us and kept seeing him when you *did* know is a major concern."

I drop my head down and squeeze my eyes closed against the burn of tears. "I know."

"But we will get over it. Eventually. Because we're family."

Those last three words have my heart finally beating again. His hands drop from me, and he returns to his chair.

Savage nods his agreement. "I'd be lying if I said I wasn't a little pissed. But I think everyone in this room understands that mistakes can be made, especially when the heart is involved. Just tell us you're not going to get back together with him."

"It's over. I promise."

Something nags at the back of my mind. Something that can't go unsaid.

Tell them.

"There's one more thing I want you guys to know."

Savage furrows his brow. "What's that?"

"I do think he genuinely cares about you. About the family. And he really does mean you no harm."

He scoffs and gives a humorless laugh. "That's all well and good, but we don't want to end up collateral damage."

Neither do I.

And it already feels like my heart has taken a bullet.

LUCA

It doesn't matter how long you're in this business. It doesn't matter how many times someone you know dies or how many threats are made against you. When you walk into your office and find something sitting in the middle of your desk that shouldn't be there, a shiver will always roll down your spine, and you will always second-guess your decision to be involved in this lifestyle.

I stare at the item on my desk as I try to shake off the sudden chill. "Alessandro, get the fuck in here."

His heavy footsteps thud down the hall toward me, and I move to the side so he can step in the door. "Sir?"

"What the fuck is this?" I point toward my desk.

He brushes past me, grabs the pool cue off my desk, and twirls it in his hand. "I don't know, sir."

I glare at him. "How did it get here?"

He shrugs and examines the cue. "It's not yours?"

"Fuck, you're an idiot. When have you ever seen me with a pool cue?"

The last time I held one was that first night with Byron at The Back Pocket. With him bent over the table and me sidled up behind him. The start of a night that led to so much more.

Alessandro flinches and finally looks a little sheepish. "Sir, someone must've gotten in last night."

"And how the hell would that happen? Who was on duty last night?"

He scratches the side of his head. "I think Frank."

I slam my hand against the door. "Well, fucking go get him!"

He sets the cue down on the desk and pushes past me out the door. I step into my office and clench my fists at my sides.

This is a message. A clear one.

Someone knows.

About me.

About The Back Pocket.

Probably about Byron.

The fact that Byron ended things and we aren't together anymore won't matter. He's just as much of a target. And I brought it on him. I'm the one who kept forcing things, kept making him examine his feelings about it and trying to convince him this was good for us.

I was the one overlooking and ignoring the dangers in favor of selfish needs.

And I'd do it all over again. In a fucking heartbeat. Because I miss him. More than I've missed anyone or anything in my entire fucking life. It took every ounce of willpower I possess to walk away from him that night, to give him what he wanted when what *I* wanted was to rage and argue with him about what a shit decision he was making.

Part of me hoped he would come crawling back the way he had for weeks, but he didn't. He said he was done, and he's kept his promise. I thought maybe the article coming out would help him see I'm not such a bad guy, but so far, it's been crickets.

I pull out my phone and pull up our last text message from weeks ago. Before that night I let him take control. Before that night he fucked me and demanded I leave. Before that night he fucking broke a heart I thought was dead and black.

My fingers fly over the screen.

< **I miss you.** >

Only seconds pass before those three little bubbles pop up. My heart stops, and I hold my breath. At least he's responding. That's a good sign.

> **I can't.** <

I release a rush of breath and fight the desire to chuck my phone across the room. That man has no idea what he's done to me. What a fucking mess I've become since he left me. And now, he's in danger even when he tries to stay away.

Frank appears in the door. "You wanted to see me, sir?"

I lean back against my desk to face him. "You were on duty last night."

He stands with his hands crossed at his lower back. "Yes, sir."

"And all was quiet?"

"Yes, sir."

"No alarms? Nobody here?"

He clears his throat and shakes his head. "All was quiet."

"Then, explain to me how someone got in and placed something on my desk."

His eyes widen, and he glances behind me at the offending item. "I don't know, sir."

"You don't know?" I have morons working for me. No wonder the Abello empire crumbled. If these are the kind of people who worked for Dom.

"And you remained here at the building the entire shift?"

The man swallows thickly and nods. "Yes, here the whole time, sir."

He's lying. And he's not very good at it.

"No chance you snuck away to meet a woman, perhaps for a little while?" I raise an eyebrow at him and wait for a response.

Men stronger than him have withered under my stare. It's only a matter of time before he caves, too.

He shifts nervously and avoids eye contact. "No-no, sir."

"Should I check the surveillance cameras?" I'm going to anyway to see if they caught who might have brought this in. It's so much easier to fight an enemy when you've seen his face. Though anyone clever enough to get in here would also be smart enough not to leave a traceable trail back to himself.

His head jerks up, and his eyes meet mine. "I turned them off."

I raise my eyebrows. "Why would you do that if you were here the whole time alone?"

He shifts nervously. "I didn't leave, but a woman may have come to visit me for a while."

Fucking men, always thinking with their dicks. It will undoubtedly be man's downfall.

"How long were the cameras off?"

He offers me a shrug, as if his failure didn't expose us all, expose *me* to a major threat. "An hour, maybe an hour and a half."

More than enough time to get in and get out.

"And you didn't hear anything during that time?"

His face reddens. "Sir, I was otherwise engaged and wasn't really paying attention."

"That's what I thought."

It's no secret Castillo has been looking for a weakness. A hole. A way to get to me. It had to be Castillo who did this. The woman was probably a plant designed to distract the guard.

"Have you known this woman long?"

He narrows his eyes. "We just met a few days ago."

Cazzo. Fucking hell.

"That's all. Go back to your post."

I'll have Alessandro deal with him later. Right now, I need to figure out what to do. I could confront Castillo, or I could make a move. Answer back to show him I don't bend to threats.

The first might be more diplomatic. The second is probably what Dom would have done. Both have pitfalls.

No one ever said this job was easy.

12

ONE MONTH LATER

BYRON

"You're back." The same bartender who was here the night I met Luca saunters over to the end of the bar as I slide onto the stool.

I can't believe he remembers me.

It was one night. Months ago. And he must see hundreds of new faces every week.

I flash him a smile, even though it's forced. I can't even remember the last time I had a genuine one. "I'm back."

He gives me a lopsided grin and scans the bar. "Where's your friend from last time?"

I bark out a sardonic laugh and shake my head. "I don't know."

That's probably a pretty normal answer around here. It may not be the typical pickup joint, but there's no doubt I wasn't the first guy to go home with somebody he met here. And most of those are probably just one-night stands.

I guarantee none of them were as complicated as Luca and me.

In the time since we've been apart, I've tried so damn hard to focus on fixing things with the Hawkes rather than dwelling on what I had and what I feel for the man who caused so much discontent.

"What can I get for you?"

"A beer sounds good, but I'm going to need something stronger tonight. Ardbeg."

He nods his head back toward the wall of alcohol. "You want the good stuff?"

One of the bottles up there is a twenty-two-year single malt. It will hurt my wallet, but it will taste amazing and give me exactly what I need tonight. A way to escape my own head.

"Why the hell not?"

"Neat?"

I nod. "Is there any other way?"

He chuckles as he grabs a glass and pours the amber liquid into it. Far more than he should.

"That's a pretty generous pour."

He grins at me. "You look like you could use it."

Isn't that the truth?

Coming clean to everyone about what had been going on with Luca and me wasn't easy, and the reception I got wasn't one-hundred percent honest.

They know me. They trust me. They don't want to lose me as an employee. They don't want to say or do anything that's going to set me off to potentially leave them. But at the same time, they're clearly lying about how they feel about the situation. No matter how much they say I mean to them, I betrayed them. Simple. That's not something someone gets over right away. So, things have been nothing but strained between all of us since I revealed what happened.

Even the opening of THREE, which should have been a beautiful event, was tainted by my betrayal. I couldn't even bring myself to go because of the tension still there. I didn't want to ruin their joy, their way of starting fresh, by being there and reminding them of the Abellos.

I raise my glass to my lips and take a sip of the smoky liquid. The flavors dance across my tongue and burn my throat. Pool balls crack behind me, and I look over my shoulder. A younger guy leans over the table with his cue to lineup the next shot as an older gentleman stands behind him, admiring his very tight jeans.

I can't help the tiny grin that plays at the corners of my mouth.

The younger guy knows exactly what he's doing. He wiggles his butt farther out toward the older man, intentionally rubbing against him. The older man leans down over him and whispers something into his ear that has the younger man turning red before totally flubbing his shot. The older man laughs, smacks him on the ass, and walks around to take his turn.

My bartender friend laughs. "Those two have been together for a year and still joke around like they're damn newlyweds or something."

Having something like that, a partner, someone to come home to every night, is something I never thought was possible when I left Salt Lake City, but lately, I find myself craving it more and more.

Too bad it can never be with the man I want. Not when that means choosing between the Hawkes and him.

I drop my elbows down onto the bar top and swirl my drink while I stare into it. The door to the place opens and closes across the room behind me, and the bartender taps me on the arm.

"What?" I crane my head around, and my eyes meet familiar dark ones.

Luca. What the hell is he doing here?

He can't be seen in this place. Now that the article has been published, everyone is going to recognize him.

The bartender leans down to me. "You know, if I had known who he was then, I probably would've watched what I was saying a little bit more carefully."

No shit.

Luca pulls out the stool next to me, the same one where he sat that night. He nods at the bartender. "I'll have whatever he's having."

"How do you know it's up to your standards?" The words come out a little harsher than I intend, but he's the last person I need to see right now. Not when he's the only one I want to see and know I shouldn't.

He barks out a laugh and leans in until his lips brush my ear. "Because I know you have excellent taste."

His warm breath fluttering over my skin has my cock stirring to life for him. Memories of him have been the only thing that have managed to accomplish that since the night he left my place. The night I kicked him out and ended things.

I raise an eyebrow at him. "According to whom?"

The Hawkes think I have about the worst taste in men possible. Of all the gay men in the city, the one I fall for has to be Luca Abello.

Fuck me.

I toss back the last of my drink as the bartender sets Luca's in front of him. "What are you doing here? You know this is really dangerous."

Luca lets his shoulders rise and fall as he brings the glass to his lips and sips it. "My entire life is dangerous, and I needed to talk to you."

"There's nothing to talk about. This cannot happen. Not anymore."

One dark eyebrow rises at me. "That really what you want?"

"It doesn't matter what I want anymore."

It never has.

"That's a pretty shitty way to live your life. Making other people happy at your own expense."

"Maybe it's true, but Hawkes aren't just people. They're my family."

He considers me for a moment. "If they're really your family, they should support you no matter who you're with."

I growl and turn toward him. "That's not fair. There's a history."

"Not with me. Everyone needs to stop confusing what my father did with what I'm doing. I'm not him." He takes a sip of his drink and nods toward my empty glass. "You going to have another one?"

I shake my head and slide off the stool. I grab my wallet and toss a hundred bucks on the bar top for the bartender.

He walks back over to us and looks down. "That's too much."

"Don't worry about it. I gotta take off."

"So, you're running from me now?"

I scoff and throw up my hands. "What the hell do you want me to do, Luca?"

He turns on the stool to face me. "I want you to be a fucking man and take what you want."

"Fuck you." I storm across the bar and let the door slam shut behind me. The cooling night air doesn't help the blistering heat tightening my skin or the anger rising in my blood.

Luca Abello can go fuck himself.

LUCA

It probably makes me a really sick fuck to get turned on so much by seeing Byron so upset. It's not his distress, though. It's the fire in him, the passion...probably because I know what he can do with that under other circumstances.

Coming here was stupid. I knew it when I got the call from my man who has been following Byron since Castillo dropped the threat on my desk. But when I heard Byron was at The Back Pocket, I couldn't resist the chance to see him, the opportunity to reconnect at the place we first met. When I was Steele and he was just a hot guy at a bar.

I never intended to argue with him again, the same argument we've had a dozen times. But I couldn't bite my tongue, not with him sitting right there next to me.

I grab a hundred-dollar bill from my wallet, toss it on the bar top, take one more sip and make my way across the bar, past a couple playing pool who watch me with interest, and out the door after Byron.

Footsteps echo down the alley at the side of the building that leads to the parking lot. I rush around the corner to catch up with him. I'm not letting him get away this time. Not unless he can tell me to my *face* that I am not what he wants.

"Byron, wait."

He stops and freezes before he turns to look over his shoulder. I take the final steps between us.

He turns slowly to face me. "Don't do this, Luca. It's a waste of time and energy on both our parts."

"Is it?" I raise an eyebrow at him. "I don't feel like it is. You need to be able to compartmentalize things better."

He throws up his hands and scoffs. "Compartmentalize? Jesus, you have no fucking clue, do you? I suffered just as much as the Hawkes with what your father did. Ben was my friend. So was

Caleb. He killed them, destroyed the club, not to mention what he did to Stone. That trauma has fucked him up so badly, who knows if he'll ever fully recover from it."

I cringe at his words. Because he's right. Dom did destroy their lives and Stone's at a very young age. It could've been me. Had I shown any interest in joining the family business back then, and if he hadn't suspected I was gay, that would have been me in that warehouse with Dom. Me with the gun in my hand. Me firing the shot that sent the Hawkes' and Erikssons' worlds into a spiral.

Ironic that I consider myself lucky to have made it without that kind of trauma as a child, yet I went and willingly put myself into it as an adult. Maybe not the slickest move. But it is what it is. It's my reality, and I can't get out of it now without risking more than my life.

And I can't walk away from the man in front of me without losing something even more important. He needs to know that before he closes the final door on us.

Byron stares at me, his hands hanging limply at his sides. He shakes his head. "This thing between us," he motions between us, "it's bad for both of us. I'm going to lose my friends, and you could potentially lose your life if anyone found out."

We both could, but that's true regardless if we're together or not, which is why I've had security on him non-stop.

I shrug. "Some things are more important."

He scoffs. "What's more important than your life?"

You!

The word is on the tip of my tongue, but I can't manage to say it. Not now. We barely know each other in the grand scheme of things, yet it was the first word that came into my mind, the first thing in my heart when he asked the question.

I close the distance between us and grab the front of his shirt to jerk him against me before I press my lips to his in a brutal kiss. One I hope answers his question. His hands come up to hold my face, and he returns the kiss. My heart soars. He's not pushing me away. At least, not yet, but I steel myself for the potential of just that while I savor the familiar taste of his lips and tongue.

Squealing tires at that end of the alley have us pulling apart and looking to the left. A black SUV slows, and dark metal flashes in the open windows.

Bang. Bang. Bang.

"No!" My cry rings out and echoes against the brick alley with the gunshots.

Byron gasps and clutches his chest before my brain can even process what just happened. He drops to his knees and then onto his back on the dirty pavement.

The SUV speeds away around the side of The Back Pocket, and blood spreads on Byron's right side.

"Jesus Christ." I drop to my knees and press my hand over his on top of the wound.

That wasn't an accident or random violence. That was a goddamn drive-by assassination attempt. And they were aiming for me. Byron just got caught in the crossfire.

He's right.

This is dangerous to both of us. Far more so than I want to admit. I thought I could keep him safe. I thought my men could protect him even if we weren't together, but that was a pipe dream. And the tightening in my chest tells me I'm in far more trouble with Byron than I ever imagined.

"Hold on, stay with me. Don't you fucking leave me again."

His eyelids flutter closed, and I use my free hand to grab his face.

"No!"

Pounding footsteps echo through the alley behind me.

"Mr. Abello, is everything all right?"

I glance over my shoulder at the useless man I had following

Byron in a fruitless attempt to keep him safe. "Does everything look all right, you fucking idiot? Call an ambulance *now!*"

Byron coughs and winces before turning his face toward me.

I slap his cheek. "Open your eyes, Byron. Look at me."

His eyelids flutter, and his slitted dark eyes meet mine.

"Don't. You. Fucking. Leave. Me."

13

LUCA

"This is your fault, you know." Savage's words are low and meant only for me. The truth of them slices through every fiber of my being and straight to my already shattered heart.

The people milling around us don't even glance in our direction. They have more important things to worry about if they're here.

I heave out a sigh and drop my head down into my hands for the hundredth time since arriving here hours ago and called Savage to tell him what happened. "I know."

It is all my fault. My fault for pushing Byron to choose me. My fault for going to the bar, knowing Castillo was actively looking for a way to take me out. My fault for ever thinking I could have anything as good in my life as Byron.

Men like me don't get to have someone like Byron. He's good. Truly good. A genuinely caring and kind person who wouldn't wish harm on anyone. The polar opposite of me. I've hurt people. I've killed. I've done things that will send me straight to Hell on

Judgment Day. We are oil and water. Never meant to mix. Never meant to stay together.

Yet I forced it.

I forced him.

I put him here.

My chest tightens, and I fight back a sob and squeeze my eyes shut against the burn of another round of tears.

Savage shifts closer. "He never should have been anywhere near you. You're the reason he's here right now."

"I fucking *know*."

I don't need Savage to tell me what's glaringly obvious as we sit in the hospital waiting room. Not with my hands still tinged with Byron's blood that wouldn't completely wash off once the paramedics pulled me away from him. Not when I haven't been able to take a full breath since the moment those shots were fired. Not when tears have been falling for the first time since I can even remember, for the man who took a fucking bullet because he was with *me*.

I sniff and scrub my hands over my face.

He's fine.

I just keep telling myself that over and over again.

He's going to be okay.

The bullet went through and missed any vital organs, but seeing him on the ground, bleeding like that was enough to steal my breath and make my heart stop. It should have been me. It should have been *me*.

I turn my head toward Savage. I hadn't even noticed him come into the waiting area until he settled right next to me. "Where is everyone else?"

He considers me for a moment, then tilts his head toward the front reception area. "I told them to wait. I didn't want to create a major scene here. I updated them already, so they know he's okay."

A major scene.

It would have been. All the Hawkes attacking me at once for what I did.

I shake my head and meet Savage's eyes. Maybe if I'm looking right at him, he'll be able to see the truth of what I'm about to say. "I know you're not going to believe me, but I care about him. I *more* than care about him."

I fucking love him.

And that's more terrifying than any threat being made against me, any gun being shoved against my head. It's why I've been so damn reluctant to admit it to myself, let alone him.

Silence greets me instead of a laugh or Savage calling me a liar. Both of which I expected. Both of which would be appropriate given my history, given *our* history.

Instead, he releases a deep sigh and shoves his hand through his thick dark hair. "You have no idea the position you put him in, that you've put us in."

I bark out a laugh that doesn't hold an ounce of humor. "But I do. Believe me, I've spent months considering how my life and my involvement in his affected him and exposed him to the filth of my life. And I know you guys may never fully trust me, but Byron does."

Savage nods slowly. "I know. He told me, and he's a pretty good judge of character. Usually."

I chuckle and shake my head as I drop my elbows to my knees. "He hooked up with me. So maybe not so good."

The man I once called my best friend shrugs. "Or he just saw what we were too blinded by the past to see. That you are not your father. That you are your own man with your own plan and your own way of doing things."

Wow.

Those are not the words I expected to hear from this man anytime, let alone after what just happened.

When the fuck did he get so enlightened?

"But even your way of doing things has put him in danger, and it could put *us* in danger again."

I shake my head. "No, because that way of doing things is going to change."

He narrows his blue eyes on me. "What do you mean?"

I sit back up and look over at him. "This had to be Castillo. He's been moving in on our territory since Dom died, and I got into it with him in my office a couple weeks ago. Someone left a message suggesting they knew about me going to The Back Pocket. He wanted to make a statement. Taking me out was the best way."

But he missed.

It may have been a massive mistake for him, but it was eye-opening for me in a way nothing else has been before. A way that changes everything.

He doesn't really care about me. All he cares about is power. Controlling New Orleans has always been his goal, since the moment he moved in and started challenging Dom. Dom couldn't end it. I should have a long fucking time ago instead of playing games with him and believing we could work things out without bloodshed.

No one avoids bloodshed in this life.

I just never thought it would be the blood of someone I love because I never thought I *could* love anyone. Not like this.

I shake my head. "This was never about Byron, and even if he didn't take me out, he no doubt has some sort of proof of where I was. It's only a matter of time before everyone knows and any chance I had of maintaining my business will be gone, at least, that side of the business."

Here it goes.

The thing I've been thinking about since the second Byron hit the ground. It's something I should have considered a long time ago, back when I first realized how I felt about Byron.

I should have chosen him then. I didn't, but I'm choosing him now. It's the ultimate grand gesture. The thing I hope will show the Hawkes and Byron how serious I am about making things work for all of us.

"Savage, I have a proposition for you."

His dark eyebrows rise. "Why do I have a feeling this is going to sound crazy."

"Probably because it is."

BYRON

I groan as I pull the button-down shirt on over my shoulders. Pain shoots in my side, but I grit my teeth and do the buttons as fast as I can. I just want to get the fuck out of here.

Fuck if they want to keep me here longer; I'm leaving AMA. I can't spend another minute in this place with the smell of antiseptic and death permeating my pores.

There's no doubt a shitstorm waiting for me outside this room. Luca's not going to be happy I kicked him out of here when they finally let him come in for a visit, nor are the Hawkes going to be pleased with me getting shot while being out with their enemy.

Fuck.

It only proves the Hawkes' point. Luca is dangerous, no matter what he intends, and no matter how much he may do his best to try to prevent it. People around him are going to get hurt, people who care about him. People who love him.

And Jesus, it scares the fuck out of me that I'm one of those people. Because when those pops of gunfire sounded, my first instinct was to jump in front of him. To protect him. The one they were aiming at. And I swear to God, that kiss right before had almost convinced me to give him a chance. To risk losing the Hawkes for him.

Insanity.

It doesn't matter how much I love him. It will never work. Not ever. It can't.

I grab the discharge papers and shuffle out into the hallway. Luca leans against the wall opposite my room with his head dropped down. My blood covers the front of his shirt and jacket, and though his hands have since been washed, they still hold a slightly red tinge. He raises his head slowly, and his eyes meet mine. The red rims around them make my chest ache a little bit. Either he's tired or been crying or both.

"Where's Savage and everyone else?" They stormed the ER and were frantic until I assured them I was fine and that I needed space.

Luca pushes off the wall and steps toward me. "He left."

I raise an eyebrow. "He just left me here? With you?"

He chuckles, but the humor doesn't reach his eyes. "He knows I can be trusted to get you home safely."

"Oh yeah? How does he all of a sudden know that?"

He shrugs. "Because we had a little talk." He holds his arm out down the hallway to indicate that we should start walking. "Are you sure you don't want a wheelchair?"

I scoff. "I'm fine."

I'm really not. Despite the drugs they gave me, the pain is fucking unbearable. I grit my teeth and step in front of him toward the exit.

He holds up his hands in resignation. "Okay, okay."

"So, what did you and Savage talk about?" I can't imagine those two sitting there chatting without going at each other. Volatile is the only word I could use to describe the relationship between them. Nor can I see Savage leaving me with this man willingly.

"We had a heart-to-heart. I told him I'm not giving you up, and I'm leaving the business."

Whoa.

I jerk to a halt and grab onto the metal railing running along the wall for support. I must have misheard him, or the narcotics are messing with my head. "What?"

He steps through the sliding glass doors and into the darkness of night, and I follow him out slowly. No way I just heard that right.

He shrugs and walks toward a black sedan at the curb. "Come on."

"Whose car is that?"

"It's one of my guys. Both of our cars are still back by the bar."

He's right. He rode with me in the ambulance. I hadn't even thought about getting home. He holds open the door for me, and I wince as I slide in and buckle my seatbelt. He joins me in the back and raises the window partition between the driver and us.

A thick silence hangs around us. One heavy with unsaid words and questions.

Finally, I can't take it anymore. "So, what's this about you leaving the business?"

He sucks in a deep breath and stares out the window as we leave the parking lot. "I thought the most important thing in my life was establishing myself, building an empire, rebuilding my name, but seeing you bleeding on the fucking ground tonight showed me I couldn't have been more wrong."

His head turns toward me, and the real pain and honesty of his words shine crystal clear in his dark, tear-dampened eyes. "You're what's important. This is what's important. I'm not going to hide who I am anymore, and I can't do this job and be who I am. So, I'm going to do something else."

I can't help the sardonic laugh that rumbles from my chest. *Ow. Shit.*

I grab my side. "What the hell are you going to do?"

Men like Luca can't just walk away from the life. He was born into it, had a chance to escape it, and still chose to come back. Even if it's true, how long can it really last?

I can't get my hopes up.

A grin occupies his face. "I'll continue to run my father's legitimate businesses, and I approached Savage about a potential joint business venture."

"No fucking way, and Savage is actually considering it?"

This all sounds like some sick joke. There's no way.

He chuckles and nods. "I told you, we had a heart-to-heart. I want to go legit, and I have what I think is a pretty good idea that could be a very lucrative business for all of us.

"And what would that be?"

A tiny flicker of hope blossoms in my chest.

He's being serious. He's actually going to leave. And if he leaves...

Does that mean we might actually have a chance?

The car comes to a stop at a red light, and he turns to face me fully. "Well, he and Gabe already have a strong name when it comes to strip clubs."

"Yeah...but they're not going to let you in on that. They don't need your help."

He grins. "You're right. They don't need me for their current clubs, but the one thing that I know that they don't is what gay men want."

"Excuse me?"

"I proposed a male strip club. Something that would entice the female crowd and the gay crowd."

He's fucking joking. He must be.

Or, it's the drugs.

I shake my head and chuckle with my hand pressed to the bandage on my side. "Jesus, you're insane."

He reaches out and takes my free hand in his. Our fingers twine together, and he squeezes.

My heart thunders in my chest. The dark eyes that have stared into mine so many times with lust, anger, and pain stare back with something completely different this time.

Something I've always wanted.

Love.

Oh, my God. Is he serious?

He leans over and presses his lips to mine in a reverent kiss so unlike all the other ones he's ever given me. They were always harsh, claiming and demanding, done to make a statement and prove a point. But this...this is a kiss that says so much more. It's an apology and a promise for the future.

"I love you, Byron, and even though you've fought it every fucking step of the way, I know you love me, too." He holds up his free hand to stop me from interrupting. "Savage is going to discuss it with Gabe. Maybe I am crazy for suggesting it, but what I do know is, I'm for sure crazy about you, and I'm going to do whatever it takes to make this work with you and with the Hawkes." He shrugs. "And who knows, The Steele Hawke Cage may just be the next greatest thing in New Orleans."

His lips brush against mine in another gentle, reverent kiss. "The next greatest thing to you and me, that is."

EPILOGUE

BYRON

I scan the yard for Luca, but he must still be in the house. Angelina splashes into the pool and comes up from the water giggling. Landon tosses her in the air again, and she comes back down with another squeal. I take a sip of my beer and smile. The kid seems genuinely happy—something I wasn't so sure I would ever see after Ben died.

Landon seems to have stepped into his new stepfather role easily, and Angel loves spending time with him. My chest aches, and I rub at it absentmindedly with my hand. We all miss Ben. That's never going to change, but seeing Storm and Angel happy gives me real hope for the future.

Luca steps up next to me and bumps his shoulder against mine.

For our future.

"She's a cute kid, huh?" His dark eyes focus on Angel in the water.

I grin and glance at him from the corner of my eye. "She is. Pretty good kid, too."

"You ever think about that?"

I freeze with my beer halfway up to my mouth and turn my head slowly to face him. He watches Angel and Landon in the water with a half-smile curling his lip.

"About what?"

He motions toward them with his hand holding the beer. "That. Having kids. Getting married. The white picket fence and all that shit."

I practically choke on the beer in my throat and cough. "You can't be serious..."

He's surely joking.

It's only been six months since the shooting. Six months that shifted between being agonizing and amazing as we worked out everything between us and with the Hawkes. Hours of talking and facing the realities of what our entangled pasts meant. Lots of anger and forgiveness. In the end, it was all worth it to get here today, to a place and time where we can all be together to share a meal as friends.

But what Luca is talking is just nonsense. "You don't want to get married."

He chuckles and turns to face me with a quick glance at the rest of the Hawkes milling around us in the yard and on the patio. "Why do you say it like that?"

"Like what?" I raise an eyebrow at him.

"Like it's the craziest suggestion in the world."

Maybe because it is.

Luca gave up his empire to be with me. Everything he came to town for, he just tossed out the window to be with me, to ensure we could be safe. He's given up so much. He can't really want to get married right now.

His coal-black eyes burn as he assesses me. "Why is it so strange for someone to want to marry the person they love?" He raises a dark eyebrow at me.

My skin heats, even as goosebumps spread over my arms. I

still can't believe it. Luca Abello—in love with me. All mine. And without any guilt. Everything I believed could never happen is a reality, and now, he's offering me something I honestly thought impossible.

"Are you being serious?"

He releases a deep sigh and turns his head to look at everyone gathered on the patio and around the pool. Gabe and Skye relax on lounge chairs in the sun while Dani splashes in the shallow end of the pool with Kennedy. Savage has his phone raised, snapping pictures like the proud father and husband he truly is. Stone sits under the overhang in the shade, looking on while Nora holds a sleeping Isaac. Saint and Caroline huddle together in the corner near the door to the house, and he leans down and whispers something in her ear that has her blushing ten shades of red.

"Look around you, Byron. Everyone here is blissfully happy. Even after everything they've been through, they've managed to find their way to the person they were meant to be with. Their other half. It took me almost losing you to understand what my priorities were." He turns back to me. "I won't make that mistake again."

"And you think getting married is going to somehow prevent you from losing me? I'm not going anywhere." I shrug.

He chuckles that deep low rumble that has my cock hardening despite the very inappropriate time and place. "I know you're not. And neither am I. But I want the confidence that the world knows you're mine and I'm yours."

There's the honest answer. Luca wants the world to know he owns me.

Before Luca, that would have pissed me the fuck off. Having someone stake a claim. Yet with him, I'm okay with it. His possessive and demanding nature is one of the things I love about him. Even though it drives me nuts sometimes, even though we argue and fight about stupid shit because neither of us wants to give an inch. At the end of the day, he's the one I come home to. He's the one whose strong arms wrap around me in the middle of the night and hold me when I have nightmares or a flashback of the shooting. He's the one whispering in my ear that he loves me.

Ever since the night of the shooting when he told me he was giving up the business, I've always known it was him. Forever. That everything was going to somehow work out. That he was my happily ever after.

"Wow." I take a sip of my beer as I try to wrap my head around his words. "You really are serious."

He grins at me, and my cock finally makes it to full mast. "I'm deadly serious. I want you to have all of me and what's mine. If anything were ever to happen to me, I want to make sure you get it all."

A chill I haven't felt in a long time slithers up my spine and cools my libido. "Nothing is going to happen to you."

His smile falters. "You don't know that."

He's right. I don't. None of us do.

He may be out of the business, but men like Castillo will always see him as a threat as long as he's alive and here in New Orleans, and he still has his deal with his old Jersey crew that requires he send a certain amount to them. An amount he now needs to make solely off the legitimate businesses here. All we can hope is that people continue to leave us alone to live our lives as long as we don't step on any toes.

"So..." He raises a brow at me. "What do you say?"

"What? Are you proposing?"

This isn't exactly the most romantic setting for this.

He shakes his head and takes a swig of his beer. "I guess I kind of am."

I glance around at everyone surrounding us. "Is this really the place to do this?"

A sly grin spreads across his lips, and another pull from the bottle. "What better place could there be than with family?"

LUCA

For better or for worse, the Hawkes *are* family. Despite all the history between us, all the vile things that happened due to the Abello family and what I caused to happen to Byron, the Hawkes have slowly returned to me.

I had two goals when I returned to New Orleans: to control the city and to get my friends back. I abandoned one for love, but the other has offered me more than I ever thought possible. Giving up my criminal life opened the door to the Hawkes finally accepting me back. It's taken a long time and some frank conversations to get where we are today. But we're in a really fucking great place.

If only Byron would just say yes, I'd have everything I could ever need.

Savage approaches while I wait for a response from the man who holds my heart. "Mom says the food's ready. Let's head in."

Byron and I exchange a look. He hasn't answered.

Savage narrows his eyes. "What's going on with you two?"

I shake my head and plaster on a smile. "Nothing. Just talking about how great it is to be with family on this beautiful Sunday afternoon."

The eldest Hawke gives me a strange look but heads into the house with us trailing behind him. Everyone files out of the pool and makes their way inside and around the massive table. These are the family dinners I always remembered from my childhood, with Antonia Hawke at the head of the table and a delicious food spread out in front of me.

My eyes burn with unshed tears, and I rub them before anyone notices. I didn't think I'd get so emotional being here again. When Savage invited us for dinner and said he wanted "the entire family" there, it was the final olive branch Byron and I needed, and we grabbed it with both hands and held on tightly.

It finally feels like being home.

Antonia appears from the kitchen, carrying a massive bowl of spaghetti and meatballs. "Everyone sit."

I pull out my chair and slide in with Byron next to me. My hand finds his thigh under the table, and I gently squeeze it before I lean into him and brush my lips against his ear. "You didn't answer me."

He turns his head toward me, so our lips are a mere hairsbreadth away. "I know."

Smartass.

I press my lips to his without even thinking about the audience.

"Oooh! Luca and Byron sitting in the tree, K-I-S-S-I-N-G." Angelina's playful observation has the room bursting out into laughter.

Storm nudges her. "Stop that. It's not nice to make fun of people."

Angelina frowns. "I'm not making fun of them, just having some fun."

Her mother considers it for a moment, then turns her smile on me. My heart stutters.

Of all the Hawkes, she has, by far, suffered the worst because of the man who gave me my name, and it's taken her the longest to come around to the fact that I'm no longer a threat to them. Savage and Gabe and I are going to be business partners very soon, and the one sticking point has been that Storm didn't trust me yet. But that smile tells me it'll happen eventually. It may take time. It may take years, but some day, I'll have them all back fully.

I nod in her direction, and Landon leans and whispers something to her that has her chuckling and swatting his shoulder.

Antonia Hawke stands at the head of the table. "Shhh, everyone. I have something to say."

"Oh, here we go..." Skye jokes from the other side of the table.

Her mother scowls at her. "Can you keep that sass in check for five minutes?"

Gabe barks out a laugh. "We all know that's not happening." He leans in and presses a kiss to Skye's temple, and she playfully shoves him away.

Antonia smiles. "I know, but a mother can dream."

Everyone laughs as the matriarch of the family looks around at each person at the table and finally stops on me. Now that the entire family knows the truth about everything that happened with Dom, I'm confident whatever she's going to say will be meaningful.

She sighs. "If you had asked me a few years ago if I'd be sitting here with all of you, with three of my grandchildren, and with everyone happy and healthy, I would've said no way. When we lost Sam and I was left with you kids, alone, I thought my world had ended. I got some help." She doesn't have to say from whom. We all know she's referring to Dom, but she doesn't say the name. No one has for a long time, and I think that's for the best.

The only good things the man ever did were introduce me to the Hawkes and teach me the value of loyalty. Something that he himself couldn't abide by. He betrayed them more than once for his own benefit, but I will never make that mistake. I know what I have in these people, and it's something no money can buy.

Antonia sucks in a deep breath, sniffles, and waves her hand in the air. "I promised myself I wasn't gonna cry. Anyway, I just wanted to say that seeing all of you here, having Luca back under our roof and everyone getting along for once, it just makes me so happy, I can't even express it."

Gabe stands, walks over to her, and tugs her into a hug.

She clings to him as tears stream down her cheeks, then pulls away and swipes at them. "Okay, enough blabbering. Let's eat."

Byron rises to his feet beside me. "Actually, there's something I want to say."

What the hell is he doing?

Everyone freezes and turns their attention to him. He glances down at me and squeezes my shoulder. "I know things were tense for a while between all of us. And rightfully so. It was my fault, but the fact that you all have been willing to not only forgive everything that's happened but also to embrace Luca as part of the family means more to me than you could ever know. And while we continue to work on plans for The Steele Hawke Cage and all of our other business endeavors, there's one other thing we can celebrate."

Oh, my God...

Goosebumps break out across my skin.

He wouldn't.

Byron looks down, and his dark eyes hold my gaze. The love and trust shimmering there is something I've never experienced and couldn't ever imagine seeing from someone else. "Luca and I are getting married."

"What?" The chorus of surprised gasps breaks out around the room, and Antonia races around the table and throws her arms around me. She pulls me up from the chair and kisses my cheek. "Oh, my God, I'm so happy for you."

I grin at the woman was who was like a second mother to me growing up. "Me too."

She embraces me, and I meet Byron's gaze over her shoulder. He gives me a knowing smirk.

I mouth to him. "You couldn't have told me in private?"

He shrugs and turns to accept congratulations from Stone and Nora to his left while everyone else chatters excitedly about our upcoming nuptials. Antonia finally releases me with a smile so bright, it lights up the entire room, and I reach out and pull Byron to me.

I press my mouth to his, this time not caring that everyone in the room is watching, and whisper against his lips, "Are you ready to become Mr. Abello?"

He chuckles and shakes his head. "Are you ready to become Mr. Harris?"

I pull back and grin at him. "We'll hyphenate it."

———

I hope you enjoyed *Steele Resolve*! Click here to get an exclusive BONUS SCENE with Byron and Luca on the 4th of July! https://BookHip.com/QDPPRNP

ABOUT THE AUTHOR

Gwyn McNamee is an attorney, writer, wife, and mother (to one human baby and two fur babies). Originally from the Midwest, Gwyn relocated to her husband's home town of Las Vegas in 2015 and is enjoying her respite from the cold and snow. Gwyn has been writing down her crazy stories and ideas for years and finally decided to share them with the world. She loves to write stories with a bit of suspense and action mingled with romance and heat.

When she isn't either writing or voraciously devouring any books she can get her hands on, Gwyn is busy adding to her tattoo collection, golfing, and stirring up trouble with her perfect mix of sweetness and sarcasm (usually while wearing heels).

Gwyn loves to hear from her readers. Here is where you can find her:

FB Reader Group: https://www.facebook.com/groups/1667380963540655/

Newsletter: www.gwynmcnamee.com/newsletter

Website: http://www.gwynmcnamee.com/

Facebook: https://www.facebook.com/AuthorGwynMcNamee/

Twitter: https://twitter.com/GwynMcNamee

Instagram: https://www.instagram.com/gwynmcnamee

Bookbub: https://www.bookbub.com/authors/gwynmcnamee

OTHER WORKS BY GWYN MCNAMEE

Billionaires of New Orleans:

The Hawke Family Series

Savage Collision (**The Hawke Family - Book One**)

He's everything she didn't know she wanted. She's everything he thought he could never have.

The last thing I expect when I walk into The Hawkeye Club is to fall head over heels in lust. It's supposed to be a rescue mission. I have to get my baby sister off the pole, into some clothes, and out of the grasp of the pussy peddler who somehow manipulated her into stripping. But the moment I see Savage Hawke and verbally spar with him, my ability to remain rational flies out the window and my libido takes center stage. I've never wanted a relationship—my time is better spent focusing on taking down the scum running this city—but what I want and what I need are apparently two different things.

Danika Eriksson storms into my office in her high heels and on her high horse. Her holier-than-thou attitude and accusations should offend me, but instead, I can't get her out of my head or my heart. Her incomparable drive, take-no prisoners attitude, and blatant honesty captivate me and hold me prisoner. I should steer clear, but my self-preservation instinct is apparently dead—which is exactly what our relationship will be once she knows everything. It's only a matter of time.

The truth doesn't always set you free. Sometimes, it just royally screws you.

AVAILABLE AT ALL RETAILERS:

Tortured Skye (The Hawke Family - Book Two)

She's always been off-limits. He's always just out of reach.

Falling in love with Gabe Anderson was as easy as breathing. Fighting my feelings for my brother's best friend was agonizingly hard. I never imagined giving in to my desire for him would cause such a destructive ripple effect. That kiss was my grasp at a lifeline—something, anything to hold me steady in my crumbling life. Now, I have to suffer with the fallout while trying to convince him it's all worth the consequences.

Guilt overwhelms me—over what I've done, the lives I've taken, and more than anything, over my feelings for Skye Hawke. Craving my best friend's little sister is insanely self-destructive. It never should have happened, but since the moment she kissed me, I haven't been able to get her out of my mind. If I take what I want, I risk losing everything. If I don't, I'll lose her and a piece of myself. The raging storm threatening to rain down on the city is nothing compared to the one that will come from my decision.

Love can be torture, but sometimes, love is the only thing that can save you.

AVAILABLE AT ALL RETAILERS:

Stone Sober (The Hawke Family - Book Three)

She's innocent and sweet. He's dark and depraved.

Stone Hawke is precisely the kind of man women are warned about—handsome, intelligent, arrogant, and intricately entangled with some dangerous people. I should stay away, but he manages to strip my soul bare with just a look and dominates my thoughts. Bad decisions are in my past. My life is (mostly) on track, even if it is no longer the one to medical school. I can't allow myself to cave to the fierce pull and ardent attraction I feel toward the youngest Hawke.

Nora Eriksson is off-limits, and not just because she's my brother's employee and sister-in-law. Despite the fact she's stripping at The Hawkeye Club, she has an innocent and pure heart. Normally, the only thing that appeals to me about innocence is the opportunity to taint it. But not when it comes to Nora. I can't expose her to the filth permeating my life. There are too many things I can't control, things completely out of my hands. She doesn't deserve any of it, but the power she holds over me is stronger than any addiction.

The hardest battles we fight are often with ourselves, but only through defeating our own demons can we find true peace.

AVAILABLE AT ALL RETAILERS:

books2read.com/StoneSober

Building Storm (The Hawke Family - Book Four)

She hasn't been living. He's looking for a way to forget it all.

My life went up in flames. All I'm left with is my daughter and ashes. The simple act of breathing is so excruciating, there are days I wish I could stop altogether. So I have no business being at the party, and I definitely shouldn't be in the arms of the handsome stranger. When his lips meet mine, he breathes life into me for the first time since the day the inferno disintegrated my world. But loving again isn't in the cards, and there are even greater dangers to face than trying to keep Landon McCabe out of my heart.

Running is my only option. I have to get away from Chicago and the betrayal that shattered my world. I need a new life-one without attachments. The vibrancy of New Orleans convinces me it's possible to start over. Yet in all the excitement of a new city, it's Storm Hawke's dark, sad beauty that draws me in. She isn't looking for love, and we both need a hot, sweaty release without feelings getting involved. But even the best laid plans fail, and life can leave you burned.

Love can build, and love can destroy. But in the end, love is what raises you from the ashes.

AVAILABLE AT ALL RETAILERS:

books2read.com/BuildingStorm

Tainted Saint (The Hawke Family - Book Five)

He's searching for absolution. She wants her happily ever after.

Solomon Clarke goes by Saint, though he's anything but. After lusting for him from afar, the masquerade party affords me the anonymity to pursue that attraction without worrying about the fall-out of hooking-up with the bouncer from the Hawkeye Club. From the second he lays his eyes and hands on me, I'm helpless to resist him. Even burying myself in a dangerous investigation can't erase the memory of our combustible connection and one night together. The only problem... he has no idea who I am.

Caroline Brooks thinks I don't see her watching me, the way her eyes rake over me with appreciation. But I've noticed, and the party is the perfect opportunity to unleash the desire I've kept reined in for so damn long. It also sets off a series of events no one sees coming. Events that leave those I love hurting because of my failures. While the guilt eats away at my soul, Caroline continues to weigh on my heart. That woman may be the death of me, but oh, what a way to go.

Life isn't always clean, and sometimes, it takes a saint to do the dirty work.

AVAILABLE AT ALL RETAILERS:

books2read.com/TaintedSaint

Steele Resolve (The Hawke Family - Book Six)

For one man, power is king. For the other, loyalty reigns.

Mob boss Luca "Steele" Abello isn't just dangerous—he's lethal. A master manipulator, liar, and user, no one should trust a word that comes out of his mouth. Yet, I can't get him out of my head. The time we spent together before I knew his true identity is seared into my brain. His touch. His voice. They haunt my every waking hour and occupy my dreams. So does my guilt. I'm literally sleeping with the enemy and betraying the only family I've ever had. When I come clean, it will be the end of me.

Byron Harris is a distraction I can't afford. I never should have let it go beyond that first night, but I couldn't stay away. Even when I learned who he was, when the *only* option was to end things, I kept going back, risking his life and mine to continue our indiscretion. The truth of what I am could get us both killed, but being with the man who's such an integral part of the Hawke family is even more terrifying. The only people I've ever cared about are on opposing sides, and I'm the rift that could end their friendship forever.

Love is a battlefield isn't just a saying. For some, it's a reality.

AVAILABLE AT ALL RETAILERS:

books2read.com/SteeleResolve

Then check out the Billionaires of New Orleans: The Hawke Family Second Generation Series to meet the children of the original characters!

www.ingramcontent.com/pod-product-compliance
Lightning Source LLC
Chambersburg PA
CBHW070938250626
47159CB00009B/3307